"So you don't have to leave?"

"No. I don't. And since you desperately want to spend time with me, I think I'm going to stay."

Natalie smiled. "There is nothing desperate about me, TJ. Don't get it twisted."

She tossed a glance over her shoulder. Her family had moved to the foyer, the goodbyes lingering as everyone tried to get in one last word and comment. She turned back to Tinjin and moved against him, tipping up on her toes as she pressed her palm to his chest. "Thank you," she said, her soft voice brushing warmly against his ear.

Tinjin wrapped his arms around her. "You're welcome," he whispered back as he relished the feel of her.

He placed a gentle kiss against her cheek, allowing his lips to linger there for a minute longer than necessary. Her breathing eased as she relaxed against him. He dropped his cheek to hers, the warmth of her skin sending a swift chill down his spine.

Natalie slid her arms around his torso and hugged her chest to his. He wrapped his arms around her back, his hands resting against the silk of her dress.

NO LONGER PROPERTY OF TPLD

D0957270

Dear Reader,

The Stallion family is officially back! After all your emails and messages and Facebook postings, I heard you loud and clear. But you know I couldn't give you a Stallion story without throwing in a twist or two. And what better twist than a new branch on the Stallion family tree?

My Stallion Heart welcomes back Tinjin Braddy, the brother of Tierra Braddy, wife of Stallion cousin Travis from my book *Promise to a Stallion*. Once again, it's all about family, friends and faith because there would be no Stallion story without the foundation they were all raised on.

I greatly appreciate you all. I am humbled by your support. Thank you for all that you do to show me, my characters and our stories your love.

Until next time, please take care of yourselves, and may God's blessings continue to be with you.

With much love,

Deborah Fletcher Mello

DeborahMello.blogspot.com

MY
Stallion
HEART

DEBORAH
FLETCHER
MELLO

HARLEQUIN® KIMANI™ ROMANCE

If you purchased this book without a cover you should be aware
that this book is stolen property. It was reported as "unsold and
destroyed" to the publisher, and neither the author nor the
publisher has received any payment for this "stripped book."

To Morgan Parsons
May you find the love you crave
And be blessed with much joy and happiness.
Now and always.

Recycling programs
for this product may
not exist in your area.

ISBN-13: 978-0-373-86401-0

My Stallion Heart

Copyright © 2015 by Deborah Fletcher Mello

All rights reserved. The reproduction, transmission or utilization of this
work in whole or in part in any form by any electronic, mechanical or
other means, now known or hereinafter invented, including xerography,
photocopying and recording, or in any information storage or retrieval
system, is forbidden without written permission. For permission please
contact Harlequin Kimani, 225 Duncan Mill Road, Toronto, Ontario
M3B 3K9, Canada.

This is a work of fiction. Names, characters, places and incidents are
either the product of the author's imagination or are used fictitiously,
and any resemblance to actual persons, living or dead, business establishments,
events or locales is entirely coincidental.

® and TM are trademarks of Harlequin Enterprises Limited or its corporate
affiliates. Trademarks indicated with ® are registered in the United States
Patent and Trademark Office, the Canadian Intellectual Property Office and in
other countries.

For questions and comments about the quality of this book please contact us
at CustomerService@Harlequin.com.

⊞ HARLEQUIN®
™ www.Harlequin.com

Printed in U.S.A.

Deborah Fletcher Mello has been writing since forever and can't imagine herself doing anything else. Her first romance novel, *Take Me to Heart*, earned her a 2004 Romance Slam Jam Emma Award nomination for Best New Author, and in 2009, she won an RT Reviewers' Choice Award for her ninth novel, *Tame a Wild Stallion*. She continues to create unique story lines and memorable characters with each new book. Born and raised in Connecticut, Deborah now considers home to be wherever the moment moves her.

Books by Deborah Fletcher Mello

Harlequin Kimani Romance

Visit the Author Profile page at Harlequin.com for more titles.

THE STALLION FAMILY

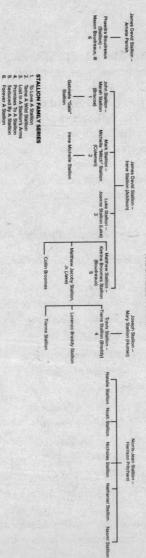

James David Stallion –
Arneta Parrish

James David Stallion –
Irene Stallion (Addison)

Joseph Stallion –
Mary Stallion (Hunter)

Phaedra Boudreaux
(Stallion) –
Mason Boudreaux, III
6

John Stallion –
Merah Stallion
(Briscoe)
1

Gabrielle "Gabi"
Stallion

Mark Stallion –
Michelle "Mitch" Stallion
(Coleman)
2

Irene Michelle Stallion

Luke Stallion –
Joanna Stallion (Lake)
3

Matthew Stallion –
Katrina Broomes Stallion
(Boudreaux)
5

Matthew Jacoby Stallion,
Jr. (Lake)

Colin Broomes

Lorenzo Brady Stallion

Tianna Stallion

Travis Stallion –
Tierra Stallion (Brady)
4

Norris-Jean Stallion – –
Harrison Pritchard

Natalie Stallion   Noah Stallion   Nicholas Stallion   Nathaniel Stallion   Naomi Stallion

STALLION FAMILY SERIES

1. To Love A Stallion
2. Tame A Wild Stallion
3. Lost In A Stallion's Arms
4. Promises To A Stallion
5. Seduced By A Stallion
6. Forever A Stallion

Chapter 1

The prestigious Westminster flat was an interior designer's dream come true. Eggshell-colored walls were lined with exquisite abstract artwork. Ornate sculpture sat on top of marble pedestals. The decor was upscale and expensive. Subtle jazz played softly throughout the space and the sound of fingernails tapping against a computer keyboard resonated in the background.

The house phone rang three times, then clicked to an answering machine on a glass-topped table. The taped greeting suddenly drowned out all the other sounds.

"It's me. I'm not answering, but then you already know that. If I need to tell you what to do, don't waste my time." *BEEP*.

A woman's voice resounded loudly from the other end of the line. "Natalie! We're headed to the pub for a pint of ale. Take a break and come meet us. I know! I know! You have a deadline. Well, screw that. If you don't show up I will personally ring your doorbell at 3:00 a.m. and kick your skinny ass for ignoring your best friends—"

The answering machine beeped a second time, cutting the woman off midsentence. Across the room Natalie Renee Stallion was seated at an antique cedar desk typing diligently on her laptop. Amusement shimmered in her dark eyes. She smiled, her grin wide and full, as the telephone rang a second time, the machine picking it up again. Her best friend shouted at the device, her deep alto voice echoing about the room.

"Why don't you have a machine that will let me speak until I'm finished? Even better, pick up the damn phone and talk to me because I know you're there. I know you're ignoring me. Hello? Hello? Natalie?"

Francesca "Frenchie" Adams sighed into her receiver before she continued. "Like I said before, Natalie, be there or I will wake your behind up. Love you. Bye. Call me on my cell if you have to," Frenchie said just before being disconnected a second time.

Natalie continued to type. The third time the phone rang it surprised her because she wasn't expecting any other calls and definitely not on her house number. Curiosity came over her. The male voice on the other end caught her completely off guard. Her fingers stalled against the keyboard.

"Natalie, it's me. Noah. Your brother. When you get this, please call me back. You need to come home."

There was a pause and she could hear muffled voices encouraging him.

"You really need to come home now," he said before disconnecting the long-distance call.

A feeling of dread suddenly washed over Natalie's spirit. She took a deep breath and then a second. Her expression changed, the easy lift to her mouth turned into a deep frown. She drew a hand through the length of her hair, twisting the silky strands into a loose bun at the nape of her neck. She stared toward the telephone for a brief moment before she resumed her typing, wanting to ignore the call that had just interrupted her.

An hour later she was still distracted, curious to know what had moved her estranged brother to even think about her. It had been years since she'd last seen him or any of her siblings. Natalie imagined that too much time had passed for any of them to just pick up where they'd left off, starting over as if nothing had happened. Because much *had* happened since they'd all parted ways. But Noah had said it was urgent for her to come home. For Natalie, home was London. Nothing about Utah remotely felt like a place where she belonged. At least, that's what she'd spent years trying to convince herself of.

She heaved a deep breath and pulled her cell

phone into her palm. Rising from her seat she crossed the room to the answering machine and replayed the message. She jotted down the telephone number Noah had left. With another deep breath she dialed it, then waited for him to answer.

It was close to midnight when Natalie climbed into her car and pulled into the late-night traffic. Across town she drove past the entrance of the Trafalgar Tavern. A crowd of partygoers was still straining to get inside. Natalie paused for a quick moment, peering through the driver's-side window for a familiar face. When she saw no one she recognized, no one there to change her mind, she sped off, guiding her Jaguar XF toward London's Heathrow airport. For the first time in twelve years, Natalie Stallion was headed back home.

"So, exactly *when* did we get this *aunt*?" Luke Stallion questioned. He looked from one brother to the other.

"And how come she had to die before we found out about her?" their sister Phaedra Stallion-Boudreaux asked.

Brothers Matthew, Mark and John Stallion all shrugged their broad shoulders. The three men turned to their cousin Travis Stallion who'd come bearing the bad news.

Travis's wife, Tierra Braddy Stallion, changed the subject before her husband could answer. "I smell bacon. Do you think you can feed me and my family while Travis fills you all in?"

John chuckled ever so softly. "Sorry about that," he said as he slipped an arm around the woman's shoulder and gave her a quick hug.

Tierra laughed. "You should be. You invite us to family breakfast and then don't want to feed us. What kind of mess is that?"

John's wife, Marah, suddenly appeared in the doorway. "Especially since the food is ready," she said, a bright smile filling her face, "so come and eat. And you all know the rules. Leave any talk of business right here in this room. We won't be having it at the breakfast table."

"They weren't talking business," Tierra said as she cradled her infant daughter in her arms. Her toddler son leaned against her pants leg, his thumb in his mouth as his wide eyes darted back and forth.

Marah looked from one stunned expression to the other and shook her head. "Do I even want to ask?"

Luke pushed past the others. "Well, you might not want to, but I have a lot of questions," he said as he led the way into the oversize kitchen and dining area.

There was a crowd already gathered for breakfast as Travis and his family followed Luke. Matthew, Mark, Phaedra and John brought up the rear.

The women greeted Tierra warmly, hugs and kisses filling the room. Family friend Vanessa Long eagerly pulled Tierra's baby from her arms. "Look at this sweetie pie!" Vanessa exclaimed as she leaned to show the new baby to her own little boy. Toddler Vaughan Long eyed his mother and the infant without interest, his attention focused on two pieces of sausage clenched between his palms. Tierra and Vanessa both laughed as Tierra leaned to kiss the little boy's forehead.

"When did you get here?" Marah's twin sister, Marla Barron, questioned. She was seated at the large oak table, preparing a plate of food for her own child.

Tierra took a seat beside her old friend, pulling her son into her lap. "We drove in this morning. Lorenzo, did you say hello to Auntie Marla?" she chimed as little Lorenzo hid his face in her chest.

Travis joined the conversation as he took his own seat. "My boy's still sleepy. He's not speaking to anyone this morning. Usually, we can't shut him up!" he said with a warm laugh. He glanced around the table. "Where's Edward and Juanita?" he questioned, referring to Marah and Marla's father and his wife.

"On a cruise to Alaska," someone answered.

Travis nodded. "Must be nice."

John took the seat at the head of the table. "I wanted all of us to go but we couldn't coordinate everyone's schedules."

"Tierra, did you meet my husband, Mason?" Phaedra suddenly asked.

Mason Boudreaux extended his hand in the woman's direction. "I don't think so. The last time you were here I think I was out of the country."

"Mason is also Katrina's brother," Matthew Stallion added as he leaned to kiss his wife's cheek.

Katrina nodded.

"It's so nice to meet you," Tierra said as Mason leaned to give her a hug.

"It's a pleasure to meet you, as well," Mason responded.

Travis shook his head. "This is why we need to have a family reunion."

"That and we've suddenly got family coming out of the woodwork," Luke said as he reached for the platter of scrambled eggs.

His wife Joanne eyed him curiously. "Who's come out of the woodwork this time?"

"We have an aunt," Luke answered.

"And more cousins," Mark Stallion interjected. His wife Michelle passed him their daughter, Irene, who eyed her father with large, dark eyes and a bright smile. "Cousins I can take," the large man continued as he settled the little girl in a booster seat and slid her close to the table. "As long as no one tells me I have another sister I'm good."

Phaedra chuckled softly as the table fell silent, everyone remembering the family breakfast where she'd announced her familial connection to the Stallion name.

Luke shrugged, pointing an index finger toward Travis. "So give us the dirt," he said as he took a bite of French toast saturated with syrup.

The former staff sergeant shrugged his broad

shoulders. He sighed. "We've always had an aunt," he started as he proceeded to fill them all in, everyone eyeing him intently. "Her name was Norris-Jean. She's actually the oldest out of the Stallion siblings."

"I don't remember my father or Uncle Joseph ever talking about her," John said. He leaned back in his chair, his arms folded over his broad chest.

"Neither did I," Travis continued. "From what I've learned she was much older and had left the family home when the boys were still very young. There was some kind of falling out and our grandparents disowned her. She moved to Utah and never kept in contact with anyone. No one knows why, though."

Vanessa laughed as she pulled Tierra's baby to her shoulder. "You people got a lot of skeletons in your closets!" she exclaimed. "Sisters, aunts, cousins. If you keep this up we might find out I'm related to you by blood!"

Mark cut an eye at his old friend and nodded in agreement. "Right!" he said with a hearty chuckle.

Luke laughed. "Oh, hell no!"

"How'd you find out about her?" Matthew questioned.

"She passed away last week and her children have been going through her papers. It seems she kept a diary. Her oldest son, Noah, contacted me, looking for my father," Travis said.

John Stallion glanced around the table as the family continued talking, everyone shooting questions in Travis's direction. Excitement fueled the air, energy like a firestorm through the space. It hadn't been too long ago that their requisite family breakfasts included only him and his three brothers. He'd married first, his wife Marah and her family adding to the mix. In a short period of time he'd seen his brothers and his cousin Travis marry, their small clan growing with wives, babies and extended family.

Last year they'd discovered they had a biological sister named Phaedra, the news completely throwing all the brothers for a loop, and now the Stallion family tree had suddenly sprouted a whole new branch. John's head moved slowly from side to side as he pondered the implications. Minutes passed before he refocused on the conversation.

"I told Noah that we would love to meet him and his family and he suggested we all fly to Salt Lake City for his mother's memorial service," Travis was saying.

"What do you think?" Luke asked, directing the question toward his oldest brother.

Everyone at the table was suddenly staring at John, awaiting his opinion.

He met the looks they were giving him and nodded. "I agree. I think we should. They're our family."

"Can everyone get away?" Marah asked, looking around the table.

"Well, transportation won't be a problem," Mason stated. "We can use my plane."

John nodded just as his newly adopted daughter Gabrielle suddenly rushed into the room. The miniature hurricane tore around the table, her deep laughter moving them all to smile. Matthew and Katrina's teenage son Collin raced behind her.

"Where have you been, Gabi?" Marah questioned, eyeing her daughter with a raised eyebrow. She tossed her nephew a questioning stare.

"Sorry," the teenager gushed. "She didn't want to leave the playroom. I had to chase her and then she kicked me!" He leaned to rub his bruised knee.

Katrina laughed. "Tell your uncle John he'll owe you combat pay on top of your babysitting salary."

Gabrielle jumped into her father's lap, a bright smile filling her face. She rolled her eyes at Collin and licked her tongue out at him. John grinned as he pressed a damp kiss to her rosy cheek. "Did you kick your cousin Collin?" he asked, his gaze narrowing.

The little girl's eyes widened. She shook her head. "No."

Everyone around the table laughed.

"That's not funny," Marah admonished. "Y'all are bringing her into some bad habits, laughing when she does something wrong. She thinks she's being cute."

Matthew laughed. "Don't worry about it, Marah. When Luke was her age he used to tell lies, too."

"I did not!" Luke chimed in as he reached for another slice of bacon.

"Yes, you did," Mark said teasingly. "And John used to wear your behind out! Gabi better straighten up!"

John shook his head, his attention still focused

on the bundle of energy in his lap. "We don't kick people, Gabi, and we don't ever tell Daddy lies. You always tell Mommy and Daddy the truth, do you understand?"

Gabrielle blew a deep sigh as she dropped her head against John's broad chest.

"Now tell Collin you're sorry," her father scolded, "and if you kick your cousin again Daddy's going to give you spanks."

The little girl pouted as she tossed her cousin a look. "Gabi sorry, Collin," she muttered softly. She turned her attention back to her father. "Gabi wanna go pane ride. Go pane ride, Dada?" she questioned, wrapping her tiny arms around his neck.

John's gaze reached out to each of his family members. There was a moment of pause before he finally answered. "Yes, baby girl. We're all going to do just that." He gave her a tight squeeze before she jumped out of his arms.

She scurried to Marah's side, her arms outstretched. Marah lifted the little girl onto her lap. "Go pane, Mommy! Dada said we go pane!"

Marah laughed. "We're going to eat breakfast first, munchkin! Then we're going on a plane ride so you can meet your new cousins."

Vanessa laughed. "More Stallions! Lord, have mercy!" she exclaimed as everyone around the table laughed with her.

Chapter 2

Tinjin Braddy navigated his way through John F. Kennedy Airport with his carry-on bag over his shoulder and his cell phone in his hand. As he stood in front of the flight display monitors, frustration painted his expression. The arrival and departure board looked like a grade school chalkboard gone awry. The word *Canceled* appeared over and over again, much like a punished student's white chalk repetitions. He shook his head as he put his cell phone to his ear and called his personal assistant.

"Yes, sir, Mr. Braddy?" the young woman answered, anticipation ringing in her tone.

Tinjin sighed into the receiver. "I'm stuck in New

York, Raina. There's nothing coming or going for at least another eight hours."

"Oh, my," Raina muttered. "Would you like me to arrange for a hotel, Mr. Braddy? Something close to the airport?"

"No. I've already tried. Everything is booked solid. A major snowstorm has literally shut down the eastern seaboard."

"I'm so sorry to hear that, sir. Is there anything I can do?"

Tinjin blew another sigh. "I've been trying to call my sister but she's not answering and my cell phone battery is about to die. Would you please keep calling until you reach her, explain my situation and tell her I'll get to Salt Lake City as soon as I'm able? When I can find someplace to charge my phone I'll call her but it's a madhouse here right now."

"No problem, Mr. Braddy. And I'll stay close to the phone in case you need me."

Tinjin smiled. "Thanks, Raina," he said, then he disconnected the line. Taking a deep breath he looked to his left and then to his right. People were crowded together, everyone at their wit's end as they tried to figure out what to do and where to go. Babies were crying, mothers were pacing, fathers were cussing and not one soul seemed happy to be where they were.

His British Airways flight from London had landed an hour ago, the plane's tires hitting the icy tarmac just minutes before all flights were diverted to other locations. The wintry nor'easter was predicted to leave some twenty-plus inches of snow in the New York area, and with half of that already on the ground no plane was scheduled to depart until further notice.

Not how he'd anticipated starting his weeklong holiday. Tinjin was suddenly wishing he'd gone to Bermuda as he'd initially planned instead of agreeing to join his sister and her family in Salt Lake City, Utah. But his baby sister, Tierra, always had a way of wrangling him to do what she wanted and her appeals for him to spend time with his toddler nephew and the new baby had been hard to resist. He loved his family and since relocating to London had missed them terribly. Despite the inconvenience he looked forward to spending some quality time with the people he loved most.

Pausing in reflection, Tinjin considered his options. With a plan in motion he headed in the direction of the terminal train and pushed his way on board. He needed to get himself from terminal seven to terminal eight. Once that was accomplished he figured he could find a fairly quiet corner to wait out the storm.

Natalie made her way to the mezzanine level at JFK's terminal eight. In the reception area of American Airlines' Admiral's Club she presented her membership card to gain admittance. Inside, the few gathered were nowhere near as frenzied as the masses in the holding pattern by the gates, and the level of noise dropped substantially. The catch-phrase Membership Has Its Privileges rang through her mind. She heaved a deep sigh of relief as she maneuvered her way to a quiet corner by one of the only windows in the room and dropped down to the cushioned seat. Kicking off her six-inch heels she sighed in relief, twisting her ankles in small circles.

She was past the point of being annoyed. Totally exhausted, she found herself wishing that she had just stayed in London. But her brother Noah had been adamant about her returning to the family fold long enough to honor her recently deceased mother. Tears suddenly welled in her eyes and she swiped them away with the back of her hand. She took a quick glance around the room and when she was certain that no one was paying her an ounce of attention she fell back into her thoughts.

Natalie had been seventeen years old when she'd left home, leaving everything she knew and trusted behind. She was desperate for a new beginning, hopeful that destiny would lead her where fate intended her to land. Life in Utah had not been easy and Natalie had wanted much more than the abject poverty that had been her childhood existence.

The family had been dirt poor, her single mother raising five children on a housekeeper's minimum-wage salary. The Stallion siblings had known little of their father, and bitterness rang in their mother's tone whenever one or the other ventured to question her about the man. Only Noah, barely sixteen years old at the time, had been bold enough to seek him out, begging for a shred of help for their family. When he was met with bitter rejection and their mother's wrath, it had kept the rest of them from ever considering the idea again.

What Natalie did know about her family was that her mother, Norris-Jean, had come from her own humble beginnings. She had been a teenager herself, pregnant with her eldest son, when she'd followed their father, a traveling minister, to Utah, trusting the promises he'd made to her. Those promises had been broken when Norris-Jean discovered the man of her dreams had a wife and another family who were more important to him.

After Noah was born, a second string of promises, which had never materialized, led to the birth of the twins, Nicholas and Nathaniel. Their mother should have known better but it wasn't until Naomi and then Natalie had come into the world that Norris-Jean finally accepted that the man she loved with all her heart had never loved her enough to want to do right by her.

Natalie had asked her mother once why she'd never gone back to her own family and it was in that brief moment that she had seen the embarrassment and the regret that had eventually hardened Norris-Jean's spirit, the wealth of it spinning in the woman's eyes. Their mother had preferred to suffer in silence than admit her mistakes and seek help from people who might have been willing to lend them a hand.

Pride had been Norris-Jean's one shortcoming and her children had suffered for it. But for everything the woman hadn't been able to provide she'd given them love tenfold, its abundance overflowing.

Days earlier Norris-Jean had slipped quietly away in her sleep, leaving her five children to mourn the loss. Natalie had last spoken to her mother right before Paris fashion week, her requisite call to check that the matriarch had received the check Natalie had been sending every month since the day she'd left home. In the beginning, some months had been much harder than others. Most recently Natalie had been grateful for the steady income that allowed her to share her wealth so readily.

A man's deep baritone voice suddenly broke through the meditation Natalie had fallen into. "Those are not good airport shoes. Especially not in this weather!"

Natalie lifted her eyes to stare at the man who was speaking to her. He was tall, lean and well dressed in a charcoal-gray silk suit, white dress shirt and burgundy red necktie. His shoes were expensive Italian leather, highly polished to a spit shine. He bent down and picked up her high heels, eyeing them too closely. She met the look he was giving her, one eyebrow raised curiously.

"You must have worn these right off the runway," the handsome stranger crooned.

Her gaze trailed from the top of his head down to the floor beneath his large feet. His complexion was the color of Riesen's chocolate-caramel candy, his eyes a deep, dark brown and he had full, luscious lips that pouted ever so slightly. His hair was cropped closely, a precision fade that complemented the thick texture of his tight curls. He suddenly smiled, his mouth widening into a deep grin that showcased the prettiest set of bright white teeth and accentuated the hint of a goatee across his chin.

"Excuse me?" she asked, eyeing him suspiciously as he waved her shoes in his hands.

"These are from Jimmy Choo's new fall collection. They haven't even hit the stores yet!" He sat them upright by her side.

Her gaze narrowed. "You know shoes?"

He laughed. "It's what I do," he said as he extended a hand in her direction. "I'm Tinjin Braddy. Do you mind if I join you?"

Natalie stared. He had the hands of a piano player, large appendages with elongated fingers. She raised her eyes back to his, not bothering to lift her own hands from her lap.

Tinjin chuckled warmly. "I'll take that as a yes," he said, not at all offended by her chilly reception. He settled himself down into the seat beside her.

"Tinjin. What kind of name is that?" she asked, shifting her body ever so slightly.

He smiled again. "It's very country, is what it is. I'm told it's an old family moniker. I was named after my father, who was named after his father, who was named after his father."

"So does that make you Tinjin the third or the fourth?"

"The sixth, actually. I come from a long line of men named Tinjin and I fully intend to pass it down to a son of my own someday. There's a lot of history in this name."

"Huh," Natalie grunted. "I'm sure that will make your father proud."

Tinjin shrugged. "I really wouldn't know. My father left shortly after my baby sister was born. We never knew him. My mother disappeared soon after that. I was raised by my grandmother." Tinjin was suddenly surprised that he'd shared so much information so quickly. He met the look she was giving him.

Natalie felt herself staring as she reflected on his comment. She suddenly realized he was staring back and a wave of heat flushed her face with color. She took a deep breath. "My name's Natalie," she said, changing the subject.

Tinjin flashed her his brilliant smile one more time. "It's nice to meet you, Natalie. So, where are you headed?"

She glanced over her shoulder, eyeing the snow that fell outside. "I was headed to Salt Lake City. Looks like I'm stuck here until this blows over."

"Isn't that a coincidence," Tinjin exclaimed. "So am I. I'm going to meet my sister and her husband, to spend some time with my niece and nephew."

"Do you come from a big family?" Natalie asked.

He shook his head. "Not really. It was just me and

my sister, Tierra, growing up. But she married into a big family and it seems to be getting bigger and bigger every day," Tinjin said with a soft chuckle.

Natalie smiled ever so slightly. "I come from a big family. Three brothers and a sister. There were five of us."

"Where do you fall in the lineup?"

"I'm the youngest," Natalie answered.

Tinjin stared as Natalie drifted off into reflection. He'd spied the woman from the entrance and had purposely maneuvered his way to her side. He figured if he had to be stuck at the airport then why not be stuck in the company of a beautiful woman?

And she was beautiful. Her eyes were pale, a shimmery hazel with flecks of green and brown. She had extraordinary cheekbones and her jawline was strong, angular and defined. Her skin was the color of light molasses, a rich, warm brown with red cinnamon undertones. She was exceptionally thin, and even seated he could see that she was tall. There was an essence of grace about her and with her light brown hair pulled into a loose ponytail, diamond studs decorating her earlobes and the barest hint of makeup adorning her chiseled features, she was stunning. At first glance Tinjin had sensed that he'd seen her somewhere before but couldn't for the life of himself remember where. Then it came to him.

"You're *Natalia*!" he said, leaning forward in his seat. "*Vogue* cover model, House of Dior ingenue and one of the most sought-after, high-profile models in the world," he added as he waved his index finger excitedly.

Natalie blushed, color warming her complexion as her cheeks became heated. She rolled her eyes. "So what are you? Some kind of stalker? Do I need to be afraid? First my shoes and now my résumé? How do you know so much?"

Tinjin laughed. "I'm a shoe designer and I spend a lot of time following women's fashion trends."

"A shoe designer? Really?" Natalie didn't look convinced, eyeing him warily.

Tinjin chuckled again. "I actually designed those shoes," he said, pointing to the pair on the floor. He reached into his leather portfolio and pulled out a collection of pencil drawings. He passed them into Natalie's hands, watching intently as she studied them.

The sketches were good; detailed drawings of footwear for the fashion-forward female. If he had designed them, she mused, then he had a great eye for heel height and lines. As Natalie flipped through the drawings in her hand she instantly recognized the pair of heels resting on the floor.

"So you work for Jimmy Choo?" she asked, duly impressed with his skills. She handed his artwork back to him.

"I did. I was one of their head shoe designers until last week."

"What happened last week?"

"I resigned. I'm moving on to bigger things."

"What things?"

"I'm opening my own design house."

"Here in the United States?"

Tinjin shook his head. "No. In Paris."

"Is that where you live?" Natalie asked, her curiosity peaking.

"Right now I live in London but I also have a flat in Paris and I'll be moving back there next month."

"Interesting…" Natalie said, her voice fading ever so slightly.

Tinjin smiled. "Give me a chance and you'll soon discover that I'm a very interesting man," he said, his tone slightly smug. "I'm also quite the gentleman. It's my European aesthetic with my Southern upbringing. My granny raised me well. I love my granny!" he exclaimed, his smile widening.

She leaned forward, her gaze narrowing slightly. "So does that mean you're a little bit of a mama's boy?" she asked. There was a hint of teasing in her tone.

Tinjin laughed. "Yes, ma'am! And I'm proud of it. There's no shame in my game!"

For the first time, Natalie smiled back. She found him amusing. He was clearly confident and had just enough attitude without being arrogant. He was direct, but not pushy and definitely quite the charmer. She liked him and his devil-may-care attitude, and she found herself curious to know more about the man.

Travis Stallion eased his body against his wife's, snaking his arm around her waist as he pulled her to him. The two stood quietly together, staring down at their children as both slumbered peacefully. He pressed a kiss to the back of Tierra's neck.

"They're growing too fast," Tierra whispered. "Tianna's lifting her head up by herself already."

"They are," Travis whispered back. "You should have seen Lorenzo on the horses today. Once he warmed up to everyone, there was no stopping him."

"He's got a little crush on Gabrielle. I saw how he was following her around."

Travis chuckled. "That's my boy! I'm going to hate to have to tell him that she's his family."

Tierra giggled as she grabbed her man's hand and led him from the room. They closed the door and moved to their own bedroom. Inside, both slipped beneath the covers and cuddled close against each other.

"I still haven't been able to reach Tinjin," Tierra commented. "That girl who works for him said he's stuck at the airport in New York."

"Your brother might not make it. I was listening to the news and they said the weather has made a mess of things. Flights have been canceled up the entire east coast. They're getting hit hard."

She blew a low sigh. "I hope he's still able to meet us. I really wanted to see him. Since he moved abroad we barely spend any time together anymore. I love my brother and I want our kids to know him."

"You know you can always fly to London to see Tinjin, Tierra. I told you that. In fact, I think you should still go and take Mama Dee with you. You both deserve some time away. I can watch the kids or you can take them with you. You know I'd support whatever you wanted."

Tierra nodded. "Maybe after I'm not breast-feeding anymore. I think my grandmother would like to go visit Tinjin."

Travis eased a warm palm across her abdomen and up until his fingers lightly grazed the curve of her breast. He gently stroked the lush tissue, his heated touch teasing.

Tierra laughed. "You're trying to start something!"

He nodded his head. "I am."

"You starting something is how we got Tianna. We were going to wait until Lorenzo was four before we had another baby, remember?"

He nuzzled his face into her hair. "I can't help it if you're abundantly fertile."

She laughed again as he continued to stroke her gently, his hands gliding up and down her body. They lay together for only a brief moment, relaxing into the soft inhalations of each breath and then minutes later both were sound asleep.

Natalie and Tinjin had been talking on and off for a couple of hours. Despite the conversation being lighthearted and easy, there was a hint of sadness behind her eyes and Tinjin felt it tugging at his heartstrings. The emotion surprised him just enough to give him reason to pause. He stared at her as her gaze moved to the window and the weather outside. It was still snowing, white flakes of ice and cold blanketing everything in view.

"So why are you going to Salt Lake City?" he asked, breaking through the quiet that had moved between them.

He watched as she bristled, biting down against her bottom lip. Her eyes misted but she fought back the urge to cry. She tossed him a quick look, then returned her stare to the window and the landscape outside.

"You ask a lot of questions, TJ," she finally answered, shifting in her seat to meet his eyes. "You're like a woman, you're so nosey."

Tinjin laughed. "You're one to talk. And don't call me TJ. My parents named me Tinjin and I like my name. It's the only thing the two left me with."

She chuckled softly. "I like your name, too, so don't be so sensitive."

"I'm not being sensitive. Just don't call me TJ. We don't know each other that well."

"I think we know each other very well. Well enough that you deserve a nickname. If it makes you feel better you can give me one. Something just between the two of us."

Tinjin paused briefly. "Okay, Gnat. I'll call you Gnat. Like the bug."

"You're calling me a bug? An annoying bug?"

He shrugged his broad shoulders. "It fits. I'm giv-

ing you a nickname just like you gave me one. We'll
be TJ and Gnat. Gnat and TJ. Airport buddies forever!"

"You're not funny. And you're a pain in the ass,
do you know that?"

Tinjin laughed. "Takes one to know one."

Natalie rolled her eyes.

"Now that you've walked all around my question, are you going to answer it?" He crossed his
arms over his chest.

She eyed him intently, the look he was giving her
moving her heart to skip a quick beat. She took a
deep breath and held it for a second. "No, I'm not,"
she said finally. "It's still none of your business."

"I told you why I was headed in that direction."

"But I didn't ask. You just volunteered it. Just
like you've been volunteering all of your business."

Tinjin smiled, his full lips bending warmly. "I'm
an open book. I have nothing to hide."

"Bully for you. I don't know you that well, so my
business is none of your business."

"I thought we were becoming friends."

"It's good they don't pay you to think."

"And you're a mean girl, too!" Tinjin exclaimed.
"Beautiful and mean!"

"You should be careful," Natalie said, her expression smug. "That's a lethal combination."

They were interrupted as a hostess suddenly
moved between them. "Can I get either of you anything to drink?" the woman asked as she looked from

one to the other before letting her gaze rest on Tinjin's face. She gave him a suggestive smile.

He smiled back. "I'd love a scotch. Straight," he said. He looked toward Natalie.

"A glass of white wine, please," Natalie said.

"And white wine for my friend," Tinjin said as he passed the woman his credit card.

"I'll bring those right over." She gave Tinjin a quick wink of her eye.

Tinjin winked back.

When the woman was out of earshot Natalie shook her head. "Really?" she snapped, her eyes narrowed into thin slits as she stared at him.

"What?"

"You're really going to flirt with another woman right in front of me? Really?"

"That wasn't flirting. Besides, you set the rules. You said that it's not like we're friends, remember?"

"It's still low of you. But then you're a man, I guess I shouldn't have expected better."

"What's that supposed to mean?"

"It means that I don't have a lot of expectations when it comes to you and your kind, TJ. That's what it means."

Tinjin crossed his arms over his chest. "Beautiful, mean and bitter. You're just a walking contradiction, aren't you?"

"Am I?"

A wry smile pulled at his full lips. "You're like an angel's trumpet."

"A what?" Confusion washed over her expression.

"Angel's trumpet. It's this incredibly beautiful flower. It has amazing color and seductive lines. In low doses it can be a highly effective hallucinogen. Too much and it's lethal. It's also called devil's weed."

Natalie paused as she pondered his comment. Before she could respond the hostess returned with their drinks.

"If you need anything else please let me know," she said, the comment directed straight at Tinjin.

"Thank you. We'll do that," Natalie said.

Tinjin laughed. "I think you like me."

"Maybe I do. Maybe I don't," Natalie said nonchalantly.

He nodded. "Yeah! You like me a lot!"

She rolled her eyes. "I'm getting used to you, TJ. Don't misread me."

"Oh, I'm reading you just fine, Gnat!" Tinjin said with a soft chuckle.

Natalie met the look he was giving her. Despite her best efforts she couldn't fight the smile that pulled at her mouth. An easy laugh slipped past her lips. She rolled her eyes a second time.

Chapter 3

Natalie had never known a man who slept with his eyes half open but Tinjin did, the dark lids at half-mast as he slumbered. If it were not for the soft lull of his breathing, with the wispy whistle at the end of each breath, she would have sworn he was staring at her. But he snored softly, lost in a deep sleep.

The length of his body was stretched across the cushioned seats. His arms were crossed over his chest, his hands tucked beneath his armpits. His head rested on a pillow beside her leg. He was so close to her that she could feel the heat from his body warming her own. She resisted the desire to draw her finger across his forehead, to tease the slight arch to his brow with her manicured nail. She didn't know him like that, yet she had the strongest urge to trail her hand across his profile.

There was something about him that she liked and it had as much to do with his deft sense of humor as it did with his good looks. He made her laugh and feel as though she didn't have a care in the world, even if it was a false sense of comfort in the moment. Because truth be told, Natalie had a lot on her mind and she couldn't imagine anything about the next few days being carefree or easy. But something about being with Tinjin had her feeling as if things might settle upright when it was all done and finished. She blew a deep sigh, a shiver running up her spine.

Tinjin suddenly shifted, his body jumping slightly as he was startled from a sound sleep. He sat upright, wiping at his face with the palm of his large hand. He swiped the sleep from his eyes, then moved his gaze in her direction.

"I guess I fell asleep," he said, murmuring softly.

"You think?" Natalie responded. "You snored and you drooled. It wasn't pretty, player."

He met her gaze. "I see waking up to your warm personality is quite the thrill."

"Enjoy it while you can," Natalie said smugly.

Tinjin's full lips lifted in a slight smile. He shook his head then stretched his arms up and out as he shook the last remnants of sleep from his system. He moved onto his feet and reached for his carry-on bag.

Natalie shifted forward in her seat. "Where are you going?"

Looking down at her he couldn't help but smile. Her nervous expression belied her efforts to appear tough and distant. Her eyes were wide and curiosity shimmered in the pale orbs. Her lips were parted ever so slightly and he suddenly wondered what they might taste like against his own. He took a deep breath.

"Restroom," he finally answered. "I need to wash my face and rinse my mouth out."

Natalie blew out the breath she'd been holding. She nodded. "When you get back we can go find something to eat. I'm hungry."

Tinjin laughed. "Is that an invitation?"

Natalie shrugged her shoulders. "Don't make anything out of it. I just didn't see any reason why you should eat alone."

Tinjin laughed a second time. "I don't remember saying I was hungry."

"You look hungry. I was helping you out."

"Just say you enjoy my company, woman! You're not fooling anyone! I can see right through you."

Natalie laughed with him. "You are just so full of yourself!"

Tinjin nodded. "I don't eat fast food so figure out where we're headed," he directed. "I shouldn't be long."

As he moved in the direction of the restrooms, Natalie mumbled under her breath. "God, I like a man who takes command!"

Neither spoke as they made their way to terminal four and the Palm Bar and Grille. They maneuvered through a maze of stranded travelers, warm bodies resting wherever anyone could find to lay their head. When they reached their destination there were only a handful of people inside and an enthusiastic waitress waved them into the space.

The chatty young woman was eager to have someone new to talk to. "Welcome to the Palm!" she greeted them excitedly. "Are you both from the city? Were you headed on vacation?"

Natalie eased into a seat as Tinjin answered. "No. We flew in from London and our connecting flight was canceled."

"It's something! This storm is crazy!" the girl exclaimed. "My name's Hannah and I'll be serving you. We're a little shorthanded and I need to apologize now because we're out of lobster. The trucks couldn't get here this afternoon."

"I'm allergic to seafood so I won't be interested in the lobster," Natalie said.

"That's good to know," Tinjin said, lifting his gaze from the menu to her face. "I was just about to order the calamari appetizer for us to share."

Natalie shook her head. "I'd look like a bruised tomato if I ate that and I'd be scratching hives for days. It's not pretty."

"I guess it'll be the beef tenderloin carpaccio then," Tinjin said.

"Good choice," Hannah said as she jotted a quick note down on the lined pad in her hand.

"Would you ask the chef to put extra shaved

Parmigiano-Reggiano on that, please? I like good cheese," Natalie said.

"No problem, miss."

Tinjin's eyes shifted back and forth across the menu. "Do you want to share the New York strip?

Natalie hesitated before answering. "Yeah, we can do that," she said, nodding.

"We'll have the thirty-six ounce prime double-cut New York strip," Tinjin ordered.

"And two of your house salads. Plus the green beans, the wild mushrooms and the asparagus fritti for our sides."

"I have to have potatoes," Tinjin said, meeting her gaze. "I need something to offset all those vegetables."

"No, you don't."

"Yes, I do. I'm a meat and potatoes man."

"The three-cheese potatoes au gratin are really good," Hannah interjected, her eyes moving from one to the other. "They're my favorite."

"We'll have a side order of those, too!" Tinjin said with an air of finality.

Natalie shook her head. "Unnecessary carbohydrates. Calories neither of us needs."

"This coming from the woman who asked for extra cheese on the appetizer."

Natalie laughed. "Yes, I did. That little bit of cheese won't hurt me. Those potatoes, however, will put twenty pounds on my hips and I make a living with this body."

"Are you an actress or something?" Hannah queried, her eyes wide as she stared at Natalie.

"Or something," Tinjin said with a wry smirk. "She's an adult film star. She does porn. Hardcore, dirty porn." He winked an eye at Natalie.

"Oh," Hannah said, suddenly blinking, her cheeks warming with color.

Natalie laughed. "Good one," she said as Tinjin gave her a bright smile.

He winked again. "And Hannah, we'll take a bottle of your best red wine. If you'll ask your resident wine steward to make the selection for us, please."

"Yes, sir," Hannah said. "I'll be right back with your salads."

When the young woman was out of sight, Natalie gave him a light kick under the table. "A porn star? Really?"

"Hannah believed it."

"I'm sure she did. But for the record I've never done porn before."

"Not even a homemade movie with you and your boyfriend? A little something for your personal stash?"

"I don't have a boyfriend."

"One of your exes then. You've never taken a nude picture for one of your exes?"

"Never. No pictures, no movies. I don't do that."

"Interesting," Tinjin muttered. "Very interesting."

"Why is that interesting?"

"Gives us something to aspire to," he said matter-of-factly.

Natalie pondered his comment, her mouth lifting to a full grin. "Not on your best day ever," she said. "But have fun dreaming."

"I can be very persuasive," Tinjin said, his voice dropping an octave.

Natalie laughed. "You might be good, but you'll never be that good."

Tinjin's bright smile warmed his face. He leaned back in his seat, shifting his legs out in front of him. He crossed them at the ankles as he folded his arms over his broad chest.

"So, Gnat, tell me something else I don't know about you," he said.

Natalie leaned forward, resting her elbows atop the table. She dropped her chin against the backs of her hands. She eyed him intently as he stared at her. A moment of silence swelled full and thick between them before she finally answered.

"Have you heard of the blog site, *Pretty, Pretty*?"

"I actually follow it. I've been following it since it started. It's grown nicely and it has a great reputation for setting some of the newest fashion trends."

"Thank you."

A slow smile pulled at Tinjin's mouth. "That's you? You're the creative genius behind *Pretty, Pretty*?"

"Creative genius! I like that!" Natalie exclaimed.

"I don't believe you."

Natalie shrugged, her narrow shoulders jutting

toward the ceiling. "Believe it. I am the creative genius behind *Pretty, Pretty*."

"I'm actually impressed."

"You should be."

Tinjin chuckled warmly. "So what was the inspiration?"

There was a moment's pause as Hannah returned to the table with their wine and salads.

Natalie swallowed her first bite of iceberg lettuce, bacon and blue cheese before she spoke. "When I was a little girl I always had to wear hand-me-downs from my older sister. She rarely got new clothes, so by the time they got to me you can just imagine how well-worn they were. But I loved clothes and I loved fashion. We'd go to the supermarket and I'd stand in the magazine aisle and pore through *Vogue* while I waited for my mother. My sister use to tease me, pointing at a picture and saying, 'Oh, how pretty, pretty! Too bad you can't have it.' So one day I set off to prove her wrong. I was tall and skinny as a teenager and someone said I should model. The first chance I had I went to New York and signed with a modeling agency. They sent me to Europe and the rest is history. But a few years ago it dawned on me that I couldn't model forever. I needed to do something else but I knew I wanted to stay in the industry. And *Pretty, Pretty* came into being."

"So what's next?" Tinjin questioned. He swiped at his lips with his cloth napkin.

"I'm all about the editorial. I'd like to give Anna

Wintour a run for her money and take *Pretty, Pretty* into mainstream media."

"So you want it to be a full-fledged magazine like *Vogue*?"

"With technology today, I'd like *Pretty, Pretty* to be the premiere digital fashion magazine and even better than *Vogue*."

Tinjin sat staring at her for a moment.

"What?" she questioned, a wave of nervous anxiety washing over her. "Why are you looking at me like that?"

"Because I'm really impressed. And surprised. Beauty and brains."

"I'll take that as a compliment."

"I meant it as one."

A pregnant pause swelled full and thick as they sat studying each other until Hannah and a second waiter slipped in to bring them their food.

Natalie's smile was bright. "So what about you? Tell me more about your shoe company."

"Tinjin Designs is my dream come true. I've been designing since my first art class at Savannah College of Art and Design."

"You went to SCAD?"

He nodded. "I did. I took a fashion design course to get close to a girl I liked. She dropped out of the class and I stayed."

"And shoes became your specialty?"

"I had a very successful menswear line while I

was in college and then I moved on to shoes for the experience."

"What was your men's line?"

"The Tin-men Collection carried exclusively by Nordstrom's."

"That was your line?"

"You know it?"

Natalie shrugged. "No," she said, a grin filling her face as she shook her head.

Tinjin laughed. "Cute."

"Actually, I do know it. Your designs walked the runway with the Diane Von Furstenberg collection one year, if I recall."

Tinjin's eyes narrowed a bit. "How'd you know that?"

"That was one of the first runway shows I ever walked. I remember everything about it. So what happened?"

"I needed to grow. I put the Tin-men Collection on the back burner and moved to Europe. After being there a month I happened into an internship at Jimmy Choo. I worked my way up learning everything I could about women's shoe designs. Now I'm ready to branch off, build both lines and expand."

"So Tinjin Designs is born."

He nodded. "It is."

"Why not men's shoes?" Natalie questioned. "Since your menswear line was so successful, why not transition into men's shoes instead?"

"Because I love women and their feet more."

"So you have a foot fetish?"

Tinjin laughed. "I like the line of a woman's leg when she's wearing a beautiful heel. I'm not limiting myself, though. I'll eventually have a collection for your body and your home. Maybe even a fragrance. There's no telling what I might do next!"

Natalie nodded. "I think that's great but your business name sucks."

"Excuse me?"

"The name, Tinjin Designs. It stinks. You know a brand name can make or break you."

Tinjin chuckled. "So, do you have a better idea?"

"Spin off your original business name. The Tin-men Collection for Women…Tin-men for Her… Tin-men Footwear…Tin-men for the Home. You've already had success with the Tin-men brand so you should capitalize on that."

Tinjin dropped his fork to his plate as he pondered her comments.

"You can thank me later," Natalie said as she savored the last bite of her steak. "Meanwhile, I'm ready to order dessert. They have a mean chocolate bread pudding with bourbon sauce."

The crowds were still thick as people moved from terminal to terminal, looking for someplace warm and comfortable to rest themselves. Heading back to terminal eight and the American Airlines lounge, Tinjin and Natalie boarded the train, pushing their way to the middle of the aisle. Natalie looped her arm around the metal pole that ran from floor to ceiling and planted her high heels firmly, her feet spread slightly apart. Tinjin moved in behind her, wrapping his own hand on the same pole right above hers.

The ride was unsteady and with the train's first lurch and shudder, Natalie's body fell into his. Instinctively, Tinjin wrapped his free arm around her thin waist to steady her. His fingers pressed against the waistband of her slacks, his palm heating the flesh beneath her clothes. He pulled her against his body, allowing her to brace her weight against his own. She fit against him nicely, he thought, the curve of her buttocks settling easily into the well of his crotch. A quiver of electricity tightened the muscle between his legs. Tinjin closed his eyes, biting down against his bottom lip to stall the sensation.

Natalie inhaled swiftly, the unexpected touch causing a wave of heat to shoot through her midsection. If she had not been standing on those six-inch stilettos she might have shifted her body from his but the unsteadiness of the ride combined with her precarious footing was a recipe for disaster. It felt good to be able to lean on him for support. She felt herself relax.

She turned her head to stare back at him. Tinjin smiled, an easy bend to his full lips. When she didn't speak, moving her gaze back to the view in front of them, he let his fingers gently tease her flesh, tapping lightly atop her clothes. Three stops later Natalie stepped out of his arms, rushing out of the train to put some distance between them. She took a deep breath and blew it out heavily. By the time Tinjin reached her side, she'd heaved another deep sigh.

"Do you need help with your bag?" Tinjin asked. His eyes danced over her face, resting on the look she was giving him.

She shook her head. The carryall felt good in her hands, almost like a security blanket for her to hide behind. She continued shaking her head as she turned an about-face and headed for the lounge area.

Once inside both were surprised to find their original seats still vacant. Tinjin and Natalie would have both bet those front-row seats would have been grabbed while they'd been gone. Settling themselves back down, both sat staring to the outside.

Hours later they were still talking, discovering the six degrees of separation between them. In London they often frequented the same spots, had attended the same parties, were acquainted with mutual friends and despite running in the same circles had never before crossed paths. The more they talked the more they were both amazed at how their small worlds had never once collided and how much they had in common. Both were fans of English football, favoring the Manchester United team. Well-traveled, they both had mutual interests in Japan and Spain, disliked fast food, reveled in decadent desserts and preferred sandy beaches over winter weather. Tinjin stole a quick glance back out the window as Natalie shook her head.

Snow was still falling. It looked like large flecks of soft cotton as it dropped down against everything outside. A line of trees bowed heavily from the weight of the ice and snow that had accumulated against its branches and there was no distinguishing grass from pavement, everything blanketed in layers of white. You could feel the aura of calm and quiet that echoed gently in the distance.

Tinjin suddenly had a host of questions for the beautiful woman beside him but he held his tongue. Something about the moment made him feel that they would have all the time in the world to learn more about each other. As if it were the most natural thing to do, he eased his arm around her back and shoulders and hugged her to him.

Despite thinking that she should know better, Natalie liked the feel of his arms around her. Where she should have been hesitant, having known him for only a brief period, she wasn't. And although that surprised her, it also felt very right to her. She leaned into his side, falling into the warmth of his body heat. She dropped her head down against the curve of his shoulder and lifted her legs to the cushioned seat, folding them back against her buttocks. Minutes passed before either spoke, both enjoying the quiet moment.

"Don't get comfortable," Natalie suddenly said.

"This doesn't mean anything. We don't know each other that well."

Tinjin chuckled softly. "Oh, it means something," he said, as he tightened the grip he had on her shoulder and pulled her closer.

She cut an eye at the man. "Don't push your luck with me, TJ."

He shook his head. "I would never do that, Gnat."

Natalie marveled at the level of comfort between them. She slipped her arms around his waist and hugged him back, looking out the window at the snow.

"Do you think it'll ever stop?" she asked.

Tinjin nodded. "I'm sure it'll start to blow over soon."

"It's so pretty!" Natalie gushed. "I don't think I've ever seen anything more beautiful."

Tinjin shifted his gaze to her face, watching her as she stared outside. He resisted the urge to lean and press a damp kiss to her mouth. "Me, neither," he whispered. "Me, neither."

Flight number 490 was boarding in thirty minutes, nonstop to Salt Lake City. Both Tinjin and Natalie sighed in relief. It had been a long sixteen hours, despite the ease and comfort they'd found in each other's company.

"Finally!" Natalie exclaimed as the two maneuvered their way to the other terminal and the boarding gate.

Tinjin nodded. "I will be glad to get to the hotel

for a shower and a bed. I'll probably sleep for the next two days. What about you?"

A look of distress washed over her expression. "I don't know that I'll be getting much sleep," she said as she turned away from him. "I'm already wishing I could just go back to London."

Tinjin wasn't sure he believed her. Something about her demeanor told him that she was anxious to get to whatever was waiting for her in Utah. And he was still in the dark about her reasons for going there. Despite hours of conversation that had solidified their friendship, she was still a mystery to him. He suddenly found himself wondering if it would always be that way.

They had promised to stay in touch, a tentative coffee date planned for when they both found themselves back in London. But Tinjin couldn't help but wonder if he'd ever see her again once they landed and headed in their separate directions. He was about to ask when Natalie beat him to the question.

"You're not going to forget about me once you get back to your life, are you? It's not every day that I like a guy who feels me up in an airport, so you better call me. You are going to call me, right?"

Tinjin laughed. "I don't remember feeling you up."

"You did," she said matter-of-factly. "I would have slapped you if I'd known it was going to slip your mind that quick."

He shook his head. "And you're violent, too. You're just a banquet of surprises."

Natalie laughed with him. "I'll take that to mean that you are definitely going to call."

He wrapped her in a warm hug. "I wouldn't miss the opportunity."

The flight from New York to Salt Lake City took in excess of seven hours. Two of those hours were spent at the Jetway while a maintenance crew fought to deice the plane and make it flight ready. By the time they made it to the runway for takeoff, everyone on board was irritated and tense.

Natalie had been able to retain her first-class seat, but Tinjin had agreed to be downgraded to coach rather than wait another half day for another flight. As he pretended to sleep, wishing away the senior citizen who'd been whining her complaints since boarding, he couldn't get the exquisite Natalie off his mind. He'd enjoyed every moment of their time together. There was something special about Natalie and her presence excited him. Her desire to hear from him again was promising, going above and beyond any expectations he might have had.

Natalie shifted against the leather seat, twisting her body to stare out the window. She wrapped her arms around her torso as she watched the ground crew flit back and forth below. She found herself wishing that Tinjin was still by her side, still making her smile and laugh. There was something about the man and she found herself actually missing him.

* * *

Natalie was waiting for him when he finally made his way off the airplane. The elderly lady who'd been seated next to him clutched his arm tightly, bemoaning her travel woes as he escorted her down the jet bridge. Natalie stood by the guardrail, shifting from side to side anxiously. Her smile widened when she saw him and there was a glimmer of amusement in her eyes when she spied his companion.

"Just don't make no sense," the older woman was muttering. "Took me three days to get here. Three days! Don't make no sense at all."

"Yes, ma'am," Tinjin said softly.

An airline attendant stood behind a wheelchair, welcoming them both to Salt Lake City International Airport. When the woman was safely ensconced in her seat, Tinjin wished her well on the rest of her journey.

"I'm home now. My son should be here to get me and then I'm going home. Don't have to worry about me traveling no more," she said. "Don't make no sense to be stranded like that for three days. Don't make no sense at all!"

Natalie giggled as the stewardess pushed the old woman down the length of hallway, her annoyance vibrating through the air. Natalie moved to his side.

"Don't laugh," Tinjin said, his eyes rolling skyward. "That was painful."

"And here I thought you were having a good time with your new girlfriend."

"I guess it's a good thing we *both* don't get paid to think, then," Tinjin countered with a smug smile.

Natalie met his bright look with one of her own. "So where are you off to now?" Natalie questioned.

"The Grand American Hotel. My sister reserved a room for me there."

"Very nice. I like your sister already. She's got great taste and she obviously travels well."

"I don't know about all that. It's where her family is staying. She married into a little money."

"Nothing wrong with that. Nothing at all."

"Says another woman who thinks a Black Card should be tattooed onto the palm of her hand."

"That's not a bad idea," Natalie mused. "Not a bad idea at all. Do you have one?"

"One what?"

"A Black Card."

Tinjin took a step toward her. "Would you be impressed if I did?"

Natalie shrugged. "Not really. I actually have my own."

He laughed heartily. "I like how you do things, Ms. Natalia!" He suddenly paused in reflection. "Hey, you never did tell me your full name."

She smiled. "I'm just Natalie to my friends and family. Natalia for those who only need to know me through my business."

"So you don't have a last name?"

She laughed, the light airiness of it moving him to laugh with her. "I'll tell you the next time I see you."

Natalie took her own step closer to him, pressing her body against his. She rested her palms on his chest, peering into his eyes. "Thank you," she said softly, meeting his deep stare. "You made what could have been a miserable trip not so miserable. I really had a good time. So thank you very much."

Tinjin smiled. "The pleasure was all mine. Let's do it again. And soon."

Natalie nodded her head. She licked her lips, her tongue tipping lightly out of her mouth. She eased her arms around his torso and hugged him gently. When she drew back, tears misted her eyes.

Tinjin drew his palm along the side of her face, his fingers gently caressing her cheek. He leaned toward her, his face a mere inch from hers. She held her breath, the air suddenly heated between them. He leaned in a second time, then gently pressed his mouth to her cheek, purposely avoiding her lips. His touch was silk, the gentlest brush of his flesh against her flesh.

She suddenly pushed him from her. "You better call me, Tinjin Braddy," Natalie snapped as she turned, moving away from him. "Or I will hunt you down and hurt you!"

Her smile was a mile wide as she waved her hand once more and disappeared into the crowd.

Chapter 4

Noah Stallion and his sister Naomi stood by the luggage carousel, staring toward the walkway for passengers who'd just disembarked. Both were nervous, anxiously searching the rush of faces for one that resembled their own. Naomi saw her first, suddenly jumping up and down excitedly.

"There she is!" Naomi exclaimed, pointing with her index finger. "There's Natalie!"

He and Natalie locked gazes. A slow smile pulled at his mouth as he nodded in greeting. Tears suddenly fell from Natalie's eyes as she moved to where her siblings stood. Noah opened his arms and Natalie stepped into them, throwing herself into her big brother's embrace. Her tears were suddenly a low sob and Noah tightened his hold as she cried against his chest.

"We've missed you, Natalie," Noah said, his voice a loud whisper. "Welcome home."

Natalie moved from her brother's arms to her sister's, the two women hugging each other tightly. Naomi kissed her cheek, then held her at arm's length. "You're so pretty!" she exclaimed. "Look how grown-up you are!"

Natalie laughed. "You've aged some yourself," she said teasingly.

Naomi swatted a hand at her. "That's what happens when you've been gone for so long."

Natalie winced. She looked to her brother, who was smiling at the two of them.

"You're home now, that's all that matters," Noah said.

Natalie nodded. "I'm sorry. I should have come sooner," she said.

"Norris-Jean didn't want that," Noah said. "You know better than anyone that if she'd wanted you to come back she would have told you so. She was proud of you and she was proud of the fact that you were able to get away and build a life for yourself that made you happy."

Natalie nodded, not sure that she believed her brother.

Naomi hugged her a second time. "Let's collect your luggage and get you home. Nathaniel and Nicholas can't wait to see you."

* * *

It felt like home. Natalie was amazed how easily she and her siblings slid into a warm rhythm with one another. The ride from the airport to the family house had set the tone, their conversation easy, the banter comfortable. Her older brothers were all bigger and louder and her sister still as protective as she'd been when they had been little girls.

Noise echoed through the twelve-hundred-square-foot manufactured home, all of them trying to give her an update on their lives and ask questions about hers. The home had been updated since Natalie last saw it. But even with the new bathroom and kitchen it still felt like the place she'd grown up in.

"Who still lives here?" Natalie asked, looking from one to the other.

Naomi shook her head. "No one. We've all moved out. Norris-Jean was the only one here."

The noise level dropped substantially.

Noah nodded. "Whenever we could, we all tried to come back for Sunday dinner."

Natalie sighed deeply. Her brother Nicholas moved behind her, gently massaging her shoulders. "Don't sweat it. Noah's the only one who was able to come back on a regular basis. Nathaniel and I are both based in Los Angeles now."

"And I'm in Arizona," Naomi added.

"I just feel horrible," Natalie said, her voice dropping. "I should have made more of an effort to come back."

"Yes, you should have," Noah said, a hint of attitude in his tone.

Natalie bristled, meeting the look her brother was giving her. Noah was the eldest, the son who'd taken it upon himself to be the father figure none of them had known. He'd protected them, supported them and ensured they'd known right from wrong. He'd been there to take care of them when their mother had been working three jobs or was too tired from working so hard to take them to the playground or show up at their school activities. Noah had been the one to see they had what they needed when he himself had nothing at all. He had pushed them and admonished them to do well. And, growing up, not one of them had wanted to disappoint Noah.

Her big brother had also supported her decision to leave Utah and pursue her modeling career. He'd given her permission to go and she had. Now he was making her feel bad about doing so.

Noah dropped into the seat beside her. He leaned forward, dropping his elbows atop his thighs as he reached for her hands. He pulled her fingers between his own as he met her stare.

"We missed you, Natalie. *I* missed you. You were our baby and our baby ran away from us. I understand why you left and I was the first one to want you to go and do well, but it hurt when you wouldn't let us be a part of your life and celebrate your successes. It hurt us more than it ever bothered Norris-Jean, and when you remember how we were raised

I would have thought that you would have known that. None of us would be where we are today if we hadn't all been there to support one another. All we wanted was to be able to support you.

"So, yeah, damn it," Noah concluded, "you should have made more of an effort, because we really missed you."

Natalie leaned forward and pressed her lips to the back of her brother's hands. "I'm sorry," she said, their gazes locking one more time. "You're right. I should have done a better job of staying connected but I promise I'll do better going forward. And I missed you all, too," she said, glancing around the room. "I did call Norris-Jean on the regular, though."

Naomi laughed. "Yes, you did. And every time you called, Norris-Jean made sure we heard about it."

"She also made sure we knew when you sent a check," Nathaniel added.

Her siblings all laughed.

"I know that's right," Nicholas added. "If you sent one hundred dollars, she let us know she expected to see that much or more from the rest of us."

"That was your mother," Naomi said, walking over to the wooden bookshelves and taking down a collection of photo albums. She carried them back to the table. "She scrapbooked everything she could find about you. Every photo of you, every magazine spread that showcased you is here. She missed you.

She missed us all, but she really didn't want any of us to come back home."

Noah chuckled. "No, she really didn't."

Natalie shook her head. None of them had ever called Norris-Jean Stallion *mother*. For years she'd wondered why. Norris-Jean had loved her children with everything in her, but the circumstances of her life had made being a mother a harder task than she'd been able to bear. Their father's rejection had broken the matriarch's heart and that hurt had been too difficult for her to bounce back from. She'd loved her children, but as they'd left home, going off in their own directions, loving them from afar had been easier for her to endure. They heaved a collective sigh.

"How come we never called her Mother or Mom or Mama?" Natalie suddenly asked, breaking the silence that had wavered through the room.

Noah laughed. "I think it was because we never heard anyone else call her that. I only ever heard her called by her given name so that's what I called her. She never corrected me."

"The rest of us just did what Noah did," Nicholas concluded. "It was all we knew."

"Hey, every family has some kind of dysfunction. That was ours but we were happy!" Nathaniel chimed in.

"Yeah, that we were," Noah echoed.

Naomi giggled. "We weren't that damn happy!" she crooned cheerily. Her siblings laughed with her.

"So what now?" Natalie asked.

Noah answered. "Well, all the arrangements for the service have been taken care of. We were just waiting for you to get here. Norris-Jean's home-going is scheduled for tomorrow afternoon and then we'll have the repast at my house right after. Tonight, though, we're having dinner with family from Dallas."

Question lines creased Natalie's brow. "What family from Dallas?"

"We have cousins who live in Dallas and they're flying in for the service," Naomi replied.

Confusion washed over Natalie's expression. "What cousins? We never had any cousins!"

"Actually, we have a whole family we never knew about," Nathaniel interjected.

Noah explained. "After Norris-Jean passed I was going through her personal papers and discovered that she had two brothers."

"*Two* brothers?"

Noah nodded. "Yes. James and Joseph Stallion."

"We have uncles?"

Naomi shook her head. "We did. Unfortunately they both died years ago. But our uncles had sons."

Noah continued. "I was able to track down Uncle Joseph's son. His name is Travis and he's married with two kids. He put me in contact with Uncle James's family. Uncle James had four sons and a daughter and all of our Stallion family is coming to meet us."

Natalie stared at her brother. "This is crazy! Why didn't Norris-Jean ever say anything?"

"I think she was embarrassed," Naomi mused. "Five kids and no husband. Plus, I did a little snooping on Google and apparently the Dallas Stallions were the wealthier side of the family."

"Even more reason she should have reached out to them," Nicholas added. "Back in the day her brothers might have been willing to help us out when things got hard."

"Well, maybe they'll be able to tell us something," Noah finished. "But we might have to accept the fact that we may never know what was going on in our mother's head."

Natalie hugged her arms around her body. She suddenly wished her new friend TJ were there to make her smile.

"So, how's your love life? Are you dating anyone?" Tierra questioned. She gave her brother a curious stare, eyeing him as he rocked her daughter against his shoulder.

"Leave your brother alone, Tierra," Travis said with a deep laugh. "These should be his 'hit it and quit it' years. Tinjin shouldn't be thinking about love."

Tinjin laughed as his sister rolled her eyes. "Actually, I'm not dating it, hitting it or quitting it," he said. "Work has kept me too busy, Tea. Although I did meet someone I liked at the airport. She's a model."

"A model!" Travis said. "Bikini, I hope?"

Tinjin was still laughing. "She was a Victoria's Secret angel," he said nonchalantly.

Travis tossed up both hands. "That's what I'm talking about!"

Tierra's head moved from side to side. "You're impossible," she said, directing her comment at her husband. "You should be encouraging him to settle down."

Hit it and quit it, Travis mouthed behind his wife's back.

"I see you, Travis Stallion," Tierra said as she tossed him a quick look over her shoulder. "And you're not funny."

The two men laughed.

Tinjin shook his head. "All in good time, little sister. Maybe I'll think about settling down after I get the design house launched. But until then I won't have time for anything else, not even a casual relationship."

Tierra dipped her head slightly as she gave her brother a narrowed gaze. Before she could comment, little Tianna let out a loud wail, twisting against her uncle's torso.

"I think she's hungry," Tinjin said. He passed the baby into her mother's arms.

"We'll finish this conversation when I come back," Tierra said as she pulled her daughter to her chest.

Tinjin held his arms up as if he were surrendering.

"I mean it," Tierra said as she moved to the door of the adjoining hotel room.

When she disappeared through the entrance and was out of earshot, Travis dropped into the seat she'd vacated.

"So tell me more about this model that you met at the airport and really like," he said, eyeing his brother-in-law curiously. "She must be pretty special."

"What makes you say that?"

"Because if she wasn't you wouldn't have even mentioned meeting her. So, I'm thinking she's a woman you're really interested in getting to know better."

Tinjin grinned broadly. "Yeah, I would," he said, his voice dropping an octave. "Her name's Natalie."

"I'm surprised your sister didn't pick up on that. She's usually a little sharper."

Tinjin chuckled softly. "I don't know if that's a good thing or a bad one. I don't know if I'm ready for Tierra to know anything yet."

"This woman must be very special!" Travis crossed his arms over his chest and leaned back in his seat.

"I liked her. She had a lot of spirit. She lives in London, so hopefully our paths will cross sometime soon and I'll get a chance to see her again."

Travis nodded. "I hope that works out for you. I really do."

"You hope what works out?" Tierra said, moving back into the room.

The two men exchanged a quick look.

"That my new business will do well," Tinjin said as he broke the eye exchange with Travis.

Tierra nodded. "What all do you need?"

Tinjin paused for a quick second before answering. "Money. I'm dumping my entire life savings into the initial collection but it would be nice to have some seed money to fall back on to keep things rolling until the designs really take off. So I'm hoping to find an investor. Someone whose interests are also in the fashion field."

"Well, you know Travis and I will help as much as we can. But you might want to talk to John and his brothers while you're here. They're always looking for investment opportunities."

"I agree," Travis added, "although Stallion Enterprises likes to have controlling interest in all of their business ventures. That might be problematic if you're looking to have free rein."

"I am, which is why I want someone who knows the industry and how it works. I just need a short-term investor with deep pockets who'll buy in while I get off the ground and who won't mind being pushed out when we're rolling."

"Well, good luck with that," Travis said as he moved back onto his feet. He quickly glanced to the watch on his wrist. "We should start getting ready. We'll need to be downstairs soon."

Tierra nodded. "This is so exciting! Actually finding family you've never known about."

Travis chuckled. "It is, but a part of me wishes it was your family and not mine."

Tinjin laughed. "No thanks, brother. If we started unearthing siblings and cousins, both Tierra and Mama Dee would be even harder to deal with. The two of them are already difficult enough."

"We are not!" Tierra exclaimed, pouting profusely. She swatted a heavy hand in her brother's direction. "You wait until I tell her what you said."

Travis laughed. "I understand, man. I understand completely!"

Chapter 5

John Stallion stood alone in the small conference room of the luxury hotel. Marah had gone to the banquet room to ensure everything was in place for the family meal. He was deep in thought when his brother Mark came through the door.

John nodded his head in greeting. "Are they here yet?"

"No. I don't think so," Mark answered. "Matthew is waiting in the lobby for them. Michelle and Katrina took the kids to the dining room."

"Where's Luke?"

"Late."

John chuckled softly. "At least he's consistent."

"You know how Luke does. Besides, I think he's feeling some kind of way about all this."

John met Mark's raised eyebrows. "Some kind of way how?"

Mark shrugged his broad shoulders. "First Phaedra showing up on our doorstep announcing she's our father's love child and now a dead aunt and cousins..." His voice trailed as he shrugged a second time.

John took a deep breath. "They are our family. We're going to embrace and love them. It's what Mom and Dad would have wanted from us."

"I get it but still, it's a lot to swallow. I'm starting to feel like we're caught up in a scripted entertainment series and someone's just waiting to drop another shoe to see if we'll jump."

John laughed. "That's a little much, Mark. A bit dramatic, don't you think?"

"Maybe, but it all used to make sense. We were Matthew, Mark, Luke and John Stallion. We knew our lane and we stayed in it. It worked for us and with you at the helm we built an empire together. We have this legacy we're going to be able to pass down to our children and now, suddenly, our inner Stallion circle isn't just ours anymore. It's just a lot to take."

"Sounds like you're the one who's feeling some kind of way."

Mark's broad shoulders pushed up. "Maybe. Maybe I am."

John nodded. He reflected on his brother briefly

as Mark dropped into his own thoughts. When he finally spoke his tone was low and even. "You and Luke are both entitled to feel however you want. Just remember one thing. Noah and his family have to be feeling some kind of way, as well. So don't make the mistake you made when we found out about Phaedra being our sister. You put a lot of distance between you and her and it took some time for you to give her a chance. You missed out on a lot of love but when you finally allowed yourself to open up, it turned out to be the best thing for you both."

Before Mark could answer, the conference room door swung open. John turned just as his own likeness stepped through the entrance. A wide smile pulled at his full lips.

The Stallion bloodline ran deep. Noah Stallion stood tall, his build almost identical to Mark's, his features a reflection of John's. He had the same rugged good looks of all the brothers, their chiseled features and haunting eyes. His complexion was a warm caramel brown, not the more-cream-than-coffee skin tone of their cousin Travis, or the Hershey's dark chocolate of John and his brothers.

Nathaniel and Nicholas Stallion and their two sisters, Naomi and Natalie, followed on his heels. Travis eased into the room behind them. There was no mistaking the Stallion family resemblance, all of them looking as if they belonged one to the other

Noah greeted him with a wide smile of his own, his hand extended. "You must be John," he said.

John nodded. "I am. And this is my brother Mark."

"Nice to meet you, Mark."

There were handshakes and hugs exchanged as the two families introduced themselves. Luke, Phaedra and Matthew joined the commotion before everyone had made their way around the room. Then there was silence, nervous energy flowing through the space with a vengeance as they all stood staring at one another.

"Why don't we sit down," John said, breaking through the quiet that filled the air.

"Did you all come alone?" Naomi questioned, looking across the table at the four brothers, the cousin named Travis and Phaedra, the only female in the group.

John shook his head. "No, our families are here. We arranged for banquet space for dinner and I thought it would be a lot less chaotic if we had a chance to talk first."

"What about your families?" Phaedra questioned, looking from Naomi to Natalie.

"None of us are married," Naomi answered. "Well, Nathaniel's almost married."

"Like hell I am!" Nathaniel exclaimed.

The men all laughed.

"Sounds like there's a story there," Mark teased.

"Someone's going to write it one day," Naomi commented. "And I plan to give them the low-down filthy dirt to make it a best seller."

Nathaniel rolled his eyes skyward. "Forgive my

sister. She actually thinks we all want her up in our business."

Mark snapped his fingers. "We've got one of those!" he said, gesturing with his thumb toward Phaedra.

"Yes, you do," Phaedra said, her tone unapologetic. "And you love it."

Naomi nodded in agreement. Natalie giggled as silence drifted back between them.

John broke through the quiet as he changed the subject. "We were all very sorry to hear about your mother passing."

Noah nodded. "We appreciate that. Our mother was…well…" He shrugged.

"I think what my brother is trying to say is that our being here, like this, now, speaks volumes about the woman our mother was," Natalie interjected. "We grew up believing she didn't have any family."

Travis nodded. "We're just as surprised as you guys are."

"I don't ever remember my father or Travis's dad mentioning that they had a sister," John added.

"From what I've been able to piece together," Travis added, "your mother left when she was fifteen, maybe sixteen years old. She was very young. My dad would have been two so that meant Uncle James was three, maybe four. They may have been just too young to have any memories of her."

"I wish we'd had an opportunity to meet them," Natalie said.

"My father died from a brain aneurysm when I was five," Travis noted. "I lost my mother a few years ago from breast cancer."

John nodded. "We were young when our parents passed. It was a car accident. I was seventeen and Luke was barely out of diapers."

"I was out of diapers," Luke interjected as he tossed his brother a look before continuing. "John stepped in and became our father then."

"And I never got the chance to meet our father," Phaedra said. She took a deep breath. "I grew up in New Orleans with my mother and my brothers were raised in Dallas."

Natalie smiled. "Looks like we have more in common than we thought. We never knew our father, either. Noah was the law in our house."

"You didn't know him at all?" Phaedra asked, shifting forward in her seat.

"Papa was a rolling stone," Naomi said softly. She threw a look at her brothers, then Natalie.

"We knew him but he didn't want to know us," Nathaniel said, a hint of bitterness in his tone. "He's actually still alive. He lives here in Salt Lake City with his wife and family."

"But Norris-Jean loved us enough for him and her," Nicholas countered. "She wasn't very traditional about it but it was love."

Matthew smiled. "Well, we're happy that we can be here to support you and to celebrate her life. We regret that we never met her but we look forward to learning about her through you."

Noah nodded. "Thank you. So what do you all do?" he asked, curious to know more about his new cousins.

"I know John's the CEO of Stallion Enterprises," Naomi interjected. "I did a Google search for you."

John laughed. "That I am, and my brothers all work for the company. Matthew is an attorney and heads our legal department. Luke manages our acquisitions division and Mark...well, Mark likes to spend our money on anything that goes hard and fast."

Mark nodded. "Yep, I do. I do."

"I had money on you in the last Moto Grand Prix," Nicholas said. "If I'd only known then that we were related!"

The family laughed.

"I'm the only one that doesn't work for the family business," Phaedra said. "I'm a professional photographer. So I couldn't help but recognize you, Natalie. I have a really good friend who shot the Dior collection last year. Your images were stunning!"

Natalie blushed. "Thank you. So you know Hopper?"

Phaedra nodded. "He and I go way back."

"It's a small world," Natalie said. "He's one of my favorite photographers to work with."

"So you're a fashion model?" Luke questioned.

"I am. I'm based in London. This is actually the

first time I've been home since..." she paused momentarily "...well, in a long time."

Noah reached out and squeezed his sister's hand, stalling the tears that had risen in her eyes.

Luke smiled, a wave of understanding washing over his expression. "My wife Joanne is a fashion designer. She's the brain trust behind JLD. I don't know if you've heard of them."

"Joanne Lake Designs!" Natalie said. "I've been wanting to do a piece on her and her clothes for my fashion blog, *Pretty, Pretty*. She's showing her new fall line at New York fashion week this year, isn't she?"

Luke nodded. "She is."

"My brother-in-law's in the fashion business, as well," Travis said. "I couldn't tell you what he does, but you'll get to meet him a little later."

"What about you guys?" Matthew questioned, looking from one face to the other.

"I'm just in law enforcement," Noah answered.

"He's not *just* in law enforcement," Naomi interjected. "Noah is the lead detective in the Salt Lake City police department's criminal investigations unit."

"That's impressive," John said, everyone nodding in agreement.

"And I play ball," Nicholas said. "Professional football."

"Hot damn!" Mark said, jumping to his feet. He pointed his index finger at the man. "I know who you are. You played college ball at Auburn. You were an All American and you won the Heisman your sophomore year. If I remember correctly your first Iron Bowl game against Alabama you went twenty-five for twenty-seven for 356 yards and four touchdowns! You were ranked one of the nation's top-rated passers and went number three in the NFL draft. The Raiders picked you to be their go-to guy to fix their losing streak, then never gave you the ball!"

Nick laughed. "Well, Douglas just retired so that's about to change."

"About damn time!" Mark said excitedly as he sat back down. "I am getting my season tickets before I go to bed tonight!"

"Do you get to the West Coast often?" Nathaniel asked.

John chuckled. "Mark goes wherever there's a game or a race. If it's moving fast or hard he wants to ride it or watch it."

There was a round of laughter.

"So what do you do, Nathaniel?" Luke asked.

"I'm an orthopedic surgeon. I specialize in sports medicine."

"Your own personal team doctor! I like that," Matthew said with a nod at the two brothers.

"I like it, too!" Nicholas said.

"You would," Nathaniel responded, rolling his eyes at his brother.

Natalie smiled as she turned to stare at the two of them. A tear dripped past her lashes as she suddenly realized just how much she'd missed her family. She took a deep breath and held it, fighting to stall any other water that threatened to rain down her cheeks.

John gave her a warm smile. "I'm sure your mother was very proud of each of you and of your accomplishments. Noah told me that you had some struggles growing up but it sounds like you've all done very well for yourselves."

Noah nodded. "Just like you, we had each other. We made it work for us." He gave each of his siblings a look, pride gleaming in his dark eyes.

"Why don't we head down to dinner so you can meet the rest of the family," Matthew said. "I imagine we're going to have a lifetime to catch up and get to know each other."

Noah wrapped his arms around his sisters' shoulders. "We like the sound of that, cousin. We really do."

The laughter ringing through the room was thick and full as the Stallion family dined in the hotel's banquet room. The menu was a smorgasbord of everyone's favorites and it was served family-style, large platters of entrees and sides for them to enjoy. The abundance of food was rivaled only by the abundance of love that filled the space.

Natalie laughed until her sides hurt as she and her siblings recalled the antics of their mother, sharing stories from their past. They were enthralled as John and Travis spoke lovingly about their fathers, the uncles Natalie and her siblings had never met. There was an air of sadness that passed between them as they thought about the men who would probably have been excellent role models for them to emulate, if only their mother had not closed herself and her children off from them. As Natalie sat there in reflection, studying the smiles and laughter around the table, an air of melancholy washed over her spirit. She blew a deep sigh.

Her thoughts were interrupted by two cherubs suddenly standing at her knee, eyeing her curiously. Both little girls were wide-eyed and red cheeked, bouncing with energy as they rested for the first time since entering the room. Natalie smiled brightly. "Hello!" she chimed softly. "What are your names?"

The older child tilted her head slightly. Her gaze was wary as she pondered whether or not she was going to speak. Her father's booming voice caught her attention.

"Aunt Natalie is speaking to you, Irene. She asked you what your name is," Mark commanded.

The five-year-old tossed her father a quick look before turning her gaze back on Natalie. "I like dat," she said, pointing at the strand of pearls around Natalie's neck.

"Thank you," Natalie said, her hand brushing against the necklace.

"You have pretty jew'ry!" Irene exclaimed as she played with the bangles around Natalie's wrist. Irene's companion played with the gold bracelets on her other hand.

Natalie smiled. "So are you going to tell me your name?" she questioned a second time.

The youngest munchkin giggled softly. "My name Gabi!" she exclaimed excitedly. "My name Gabi Stallion," she repeated, emphasizing her last name.

John laughed, his face glowing with pride. "That one belongs to me and Marah. She's been practicing her name for weeks now and has finally gotten it down."

Natalie laughed. "And are you going to tell me your name?" she asked, her gaze meeting the other child's.

"Irene. Irene Stallion," she said with an air of attitude before she bounded off in the opposite direction. Gabi raced after her bestie, the two little girls spying a rubber ball to entertain themselves with.

Michelle shook her head. "That one's her father's child. And those two together are trouble waiting to happen."

Marah nodded. "I'm going to hate it for us all when those two hit their teens. Both are hell on wheels already. Tweedledum and Tweedledee."

A round of laughter rang around the table. Natalie wasn't used to the commotion that came with toddlers and infants. She'd never been exposed to so many kids together in one room and none of her friends had started having children yet. Noah seemed the most comfortable as he rocked Travis's infant daughter in his arms.

Natalie turned to Tierra. "I was hoping to meet

your brother. Travis said he's in the fashion business."

Tierra nodded. "He is."

"What does he do?"

"He's a designer but at the moment I don't think he knows what he wants to design. One minute it's clothes, the next shoes. Next week he'll want to design airbags for all we know. I love him to death but I think he's still trying to find himself."

Natalie nodded. "I actually met a shoe designer the other day who seemed very certain about what he wanted to do. He really impressed me. I'm sure your brother will find his way eventually. Hopefully he'll be able to join us tomorrow. I'd love to talk to him."

Tierra nodded. "I'm sure he will. He was nursing a headache and I think jet lag finally set in so I told him to order room service and just rest."

The conversation was suddenly interrupted by a high-pitched wail. Everyone turned to see what had happened just as Gabi kicked Irene in the knee. Before either's parents could get to them the girls had each other in a wrestling hold, rolling across the floor with everything in them. John reached the fray and separated one from the other, the duo hanging in midair as he held them high, his look chastising. Both girls were crying, their arms flailing as they pointed at the other, racing to tattle about who had done what to whom.

The laughter was thunderous, the Stallion men thoroughly entertained as both mothers shook their heads. Marah threw up her hands as she tossed a look at Michelle, whose own frustrations spilled out of the eye roll she gave her sister-in-law.

Natalie laughed heartily as her sister gave her a warm hug. "Now that brings back memories!"

Chapter 6

Tinjin navigated his rental car to one of the most coveted addresses of downtown Salt Lake City. In the affluent Federal Heights neighborhood, homes dated back to the early 1900s. As he drove through the area he was enthralled by the mountains that sat to the north and impressed with the campus of the University of Utah, which rested to the south and east.

Cars lined the street and driveway of Noah Stallion's Arlington Drive home, people moving into and out of the residence. The brick home offered a timeless design and modern touches. Tinjin was impressed as he made his way inside. The interior design had been well planned, the floor plan offering effortless entertaining and main floor living options.

From where he stood in the front foyer he could see bold French doors that led to a shady patio area. As he moved farther into the house he took note of the marble surfaces, custom cabinetry and stainless-steel appliances. Vaulted twenty-foot ceilings gave the space an inviting openness.

Mourners mingled in close clusters, friends and acquaintances coming to support the family and offer their condolences. The mood was somber, voices echoing in hushed whispers. The repast was well attended and as Tinjin moved from room to room he was hard-pressed to recognize a familiar face. When he walked into the family room he finally found his sister and her husband seated on the leather couch, in conversation with an elderly couple.

Tierra waved him over, her face brightening at the sight of him. She politely excused herself from the conversation and jumped to her feet. She moved in his direction, throwing her arms around his neck.

"Hey, sorry I'm late," he said, his voice low. He hugged her tightly, sensing her distress.

Tierra nodded her head against his shoulder.

"Are you okay?" Tinjin asked.

She nodded. "The funeral, it was just so sad."

Tinjin met his sister's gaze. "It was a funeral, Tea. Funerals are always sad."

Tierra rolled her eyes. "Don't be snarky, please."

"I wasn't trying to be snarky, Tierra. You know how much I hate funerals. This is not how I wanted to be spending my holiday."

Tierra narrowed her gaze on her brother. "I know and I appreciate you coming. I just needed to spend some time with you. And I wanted you to spend time with your niece and nephew."

He nodded. "Well, the baby was sound asleep when I left. And one of the nannies was entertaining Lorenzo and Gabrielle. All the kids were good."

Tierra suddenly gestured to someone behind him. "Let me introduce you to Travis's cousin," she said as he turned to see where she stared.

The man approaching them was clearly a Stallion. He stood as tall as Tinjin's brother-in-law, and his features were much like those of the Texas family. He kept pulling at the neckline of his dress shirt, looking uncomfortable in the double-breasted suit he wore. He smiled politely as he joined them, his fingers passing one more time from ear to ear across his neck.

Tierra rested a comforting hand against the man's arm. "Noah, let me introduce you to my brother Tinjin," she said softly. "Tinjin, this is Noah Stallion, Travis's first cousin."

Noah nodded as he extended his hand in greeting. "Thank you for coming," he said by rote, the comment having been repeated over and over again.

Tinjin shook his hand. "I wish it were under different circumstances. I was very sorry to hear about your loss."

Noah smiled as he took a deep breath. "Thank you. Your sister has been a godsend. I really appreciate everything she and your family have been doing for us today."

Tinjin smiled back. "We're all your family now, too, brother."

Noah paused for a moment, Tinjin's words blowing warmly through his spirit. He nodded, his smile smoothing the worry lines that had creased his forehead. He extended an arm and the two men bumped shoulders in that one-armed hug men were renowned for. "Thank you. I appreciate that more than you'll ever know."

Tierra smiled brightly. "Noah, can I get you anything? Have you eaten?"

He shook his head. "I'm good, Tierra. I appreciate you asking. But I am worried about my baby sister. She's been on edge and I'm afraid she might break."

"I saw her a moment ago and tried to get her to eat something but she refused," Tierra said. She stole a glance around the room. "There she is. Let me go check on her again," she noted as she tossed both men a quick smile. "I'll be back."

Tinjin shifted his gaze to follow where his sister headed. His eyes suddenly widened with recognition. "Natalie is your sister?" he asked, his gaze snapping in Noah's direction.

The man nodded. "Yes, my youngest. Do you know Natalie?"

Tinjin's head bobbed against his neck. "I do," he said. "I can't believe I didn't make the connection."

Noah tapped him against his shoulder. "I'm sure

she could use a good friend right now. Why don't you go say hello. I have a few more people I need to speak to," he said.

Before Tinjin could respond Noah moved off in the opposite direction, expressing his appreciation to other friends who had come to call on the family. Turning his attention back to the beautiful woman who stood alone against a back wall, Tinjin took a deep breath. He'd taken his first step in her direction when she suddenly looked toward him, her gaze catching his. Surprise painted her expression.

Tierra had just made it to Natalie's side when Natalie brushed past her, moving quickly toward Tinjin instead. He crossed the distance between them and met her halfway, opening his arms to welcome her against him.

"Tinjin!" she exclaimed. "What are you doing here?"

"Why didn't you tell me your mother had died?" he questioned as he tightened the hold he had around her torso. "You should have told me."

Tears suddenly seeped from her eyes. She intensified the grip she had around his waist and sobbed quietly, her tears dampening the front of his shirt. He continued to hold her, his gaze sweeping around the room. His noticed concerned stares, people eyeing them both compassionately. He didn't miss her brother's anxiety as Noah took a step toward them. A woman who resembled him and Natalie stalled his approach, her hand against his upper arm hold-

ing him back. Even his sister, Tierra, eyed them both
with trepidation, one arm wrapped around her waist,
the other clutching nervously at the pearls she wore
around her neck.

When Natalie was all cried out she took a step
back, moving herself out of his arms. She swiped at
her eyes, then met the concerned look he was giving
her. "I don't understand. What are you doing here?"

Tinjin smiled. "My sister is Tierra Stallion. She's
married to your cousin Travis."

Natalie nodded. "I guess if I'd have told you
my full name we would have made the connection
sooner."

"We would have," he agreed.

She took a deep breath and then a second. "So
now that I've embarrassed myself miserably, crying like a baby, I should probably introduce you to
my family." She grabbed his hand and led the way.

Tinjin was only slightly disconcerted when they
came to a quick halt in front of Noah and two other
men who'd joined him.

Natalie's introduction was abrupt at best. "Tinjin, these are my brothers. Noah, Nathaniel, Nicholas, this is Tinjin," she said, "and this is my sister,
Naomi."

Tinjin extended his hands in greeting. The Stallion brothers were eyeing him suspiciously. "It's very
nice to meet you all," Tinjin said, his own anxiety
beginning to stir like the barest wisp of a breeze
through his spirit.

Noah nodded as he gestured toward his family. "Tinjin is related to the Stallions by marriage. Travis's wife, Tierra, is his sister."

"How do you two know each other?" Naomi asked, one eyebrow raised curiously.

"We met on the flight in," Tinjin said.

"So you just met?" Nicholas questioned. His stance tightened as he shifted his weight from one leg to the other, his hands clenched into tight fists at his side.

Tinjin nodded. "Yes. We were stranded at Kennedy airport together. Spent two days talking."

"So where do you live?" the other brother asked.

Natalie shook her head vehemently. "This is not going to be an episode of twenty questions for the new boyfriend hour," she said, cutting her gaze from one sibling to the next. "Not going to happen," she concluded as she grabbed Tinjin's hand and pulled him in the opposite direction.

Amusement danced in Tinjin's eyes as he quickly glanced over his shoulder, both their families eyeing them curiously.

They moved through the rear of the house, into the kitchen and outside to the backyard. Natalie didn't stop until they reached a concrete bench that rested at the edge of the floral garden that decorated the landscape. They both sat.

"You have a sister, so I'm sure you get it, but my brothers can be really annoying when they want to be. And my sister, Naomi, can be worse!"

Tinjin laughed. "I do get it. They're concerned about your well-being. It's what family does. But you have just given them more reason to be concerned. I had no issues with answering their questions."

Natalie rolled her eyes. "Well, we don't know each other well enough for you to be getting the third degree. I haven't decided if I like you yet."

"So then I'm *not* your new boyfriend?"

She gave him a look, her eyes wide, her face skewed awkwardly. "No one said anything about you being my boyfriend, TJ!"

Tinjin laughed. "Yes, you did, Gnat. You said there was going to be no new-boyfriend questioning going on."

"I did not!" she exclaimed.

He continued to laugh, his face reddening with glee. "You did! You really did!"

"I didn't!" Her voice rose to a high pitch.

"You did," Noah said, having moved outside to join them.

Natalie opened and closed her mouth like a guppy out of water. She finally took a deep breath, tossing both men an annoyed glare. "Maybe I did, but it was an accident. I'm not myself right now."

"Which is why I think you need to take things slow," Noah said, his comment directed at Tinjin. "Very slow." He turned to stare at his sister. "You're in mourning right now. You don't need to be making any life-changing decisions for at least the next six months. Any decisions, Natalie. People will take advantage of you when they know you're in turmoil."

Tinjin bristled. He paused, locking gazes with the other man. For a brief moment he wanted to be offended but realized he would have said the same thing if the situation had been reversed. He took a deep breath before speaking. "Your brother's right, Natalie. Not everyone is going to have your best interests at heart. I care about you and I don't want to see you hurt."

"So do I need to worry about you hurting me?" she asked, eyeing him intently.

Tinjin shook his head. "Never, but I wasn't talking about me." He looked to Noah who was still staring at him with reservation. "I like to think I'm one of the good guys. My grandmother raised me well and I would never do anything to embarrass her. I also value everything she taught me, first and foremost to be respectful of all women, particularly one I'm interested in." He shifted his gaze toward Natalie. "To that end, it's important to me that I have your family's blessing, Natalie. They need to like me. Just like my sister Tierra and my grandmother will need to like you, too. Otherwise, you and I can't even be friends."

Natalie scowled, her head waving from side to side. She crossed her arms over her chest as she turned to stare at the flowers. She didn't bother to respond.

Noah chuckled. He extended his hand to Tinjin. "I look forward to getting to know you, Tinjin. And good luck. She can be quite a handful!" Her brother was still laughing as he made his way across the lawn and back inside the home.

Tierra was staring out the sliding glass doors as Noah made his way through the entrance. The two locked gazes.

"Is everything okay?" she asked, concern tensing her brow.

"Yeah, I think it is," Noah said, his grin wide and full. "And I really like your brother. I'm glad my sister has someone like him to lean on."

The home had finally gone quiet, the last of the well-wishers pulling out of the driveway. All of the Stallions were grateful for the moment, each falling into thought as they sat together in Noah's living room. It had been an exceptionally long day and Natalie and her siblings were grateful for it to finally be over.

John was the first to break through the silence. "I want to invite you all to come to Dallas whenever you want. Our home is always open to you, so whenever you need or want to get away, just call. The Stallion jet will always be at your disposal. We're your family and I hope you know that you can always trust us to be here for you."

Noah nodded. For the first time since his mother's passing tears misted his eyes. He dropped his gaze to the floor, his hands clasped tightly together as his elbows rested against his thighs. He nodded but the words were caught in his throat. As he struggled not to cry, John moved to his side, resting a large hand against his broad shoulder. Noah cleared his throat and took a deep breath, pushing warm air past his full lips.

Natalie chimed in from her seat in the corner. "We really appreciate that, John, and we appreciate everything you all have done for us."

Naomi nodded her concurrence. Her face lifted with a bright smile. "It feels good to have family here to support us," she said. "This is a new experience for us."

Nicholas chuckled. "It feels odd!"

Tierra smiled. "With this clan, you'll get use to it."

Noah moved onto his feet, having salvaged his composure. He extended his arms and hugged his cousin, the two men tapping each other on the back. Gratitude seeped from every pore. "Thank you," he said, his voice a loud whisper.

Everyone in the room struggled with their emotions, the women fighting not to cry, the men holding tight to their own tears. Naomi changed the subject, shifting the conversation.

"Did you see Nolan Perry when he came into the church?" Naomi asked, looking from one brother to the other.

Nicholas and Nathaniel shook their heads.

"He was at the funeral?" Natalie questioned. She shifted forward in her seat. "I don't think I'd even know what he looked like if I ran into him on the street."

Noah nodded his head. "Yes, he sat in the back. But he didn't stay long. He was gone before the end of the service."

"Who's Nolan Perry?" Tinjin questioned, asking what everyone else was thinking.

Natalie heaved a deep sigh. "Our sperm donor," she quipped.

"Don't be ugly," Noah admonished. His gaze swept around the room. "Nolan Perry is our father, but he's never had anything to do with us and we really don't know him."

"He's never been a father," Naomi snapped.

"But he came to your mother's funeral so that means something, right?" Marah asked as she looked from one to the other.

Nicholas grunted. "He probably just wanted to make sure she was dead."

Nathaniel laughed. "He's going to get a surprise when he lays his head down to sleep tonight," he said.

The siblings all laughed.

"Why is that funny?" Mark questioned.

Noah's head moved from side to side. "Norris-Jean use to threaten to come back from the grave to haunt him if he even thought about showing up at her funeral."

John chuckled. "Well, let's hope she goes easy on the man."

"Let's hope she haunts the hell out of him," Naomi retorted.

They all chuckled, the laughter ranging from anxious to liberating. The tense air seemed to dissipate as the family joked back and forth. An hour later the Texas Stallions rose to take their leave. Hugs and kisses filled the air, promises ringing between them all to stay in touch, everyone committed to building on the familial foundation that had been established.

Tierra wrapped her arms around Natalie's shoulders and kissed her cheek. "You have all my contact information, right?"

"I do," Natalie nodded. "And I promise to call."

"If you don't, I will call you," Tierra admonished.

"And she will," Tinjin interjected. He palmed his sister's shoulders and squeezed her gently.

Tierra swatted a hand at her brother before hugging Natalie one last time. Wishing them both well, she moved to the other side of the room to hug and kiss the rest of the family goodbye.

Tinjin pulled Natalie close and kissed her forehead. The gesture was sweet and gentle, the warmth of it feeling wholeheartedly natural as they stood arm in arm.

"So, when do you leave?" Natalie asked, looking in his direction.

"I haven't decided yet."

"You're not going back to Dallas with your sister?"

"Do you want me to?"

"I really don't care what you do," Natalie quipped.

Tinjin laughed. "Then why'd you ask?"

Natalie sucked her teeth as she shifted her gaze skyward. She took a deep breath. "I was just being polite."

"It's your lie, Gnat, tell it any way you want," Tinjin said.

Natalie rolled her eyes a second time. "Well," she started, "if you're not leaving right away maybe we can spend some time together tomorrow."

"Do you want to spend time with me?"

"I know you've never been to Salt Lake City before and a lot has changed since the last time I was here. I thought maybe we could explore the city together. But if you need to leave, I understand."

Tinjin paused, pondering her comment. A slight smile pulled at his lips. "I'd like that. I'd like it a lot. I think I can hang around for another day or two."

"So you don't have to leave?"

"No. I don't. And since you desperately want to spend time with me, I think I'm going to stay."

Natalie smiled. "There is nothing desperate about me, TJ. Don't get it twisted."

She glanced over her shoulder. Her family had moved to the foyer, the goodbyes lingering as everyone tried to get in one last word and comment. She turned back to Tinjin and moved against him, tipping up on her toes as she pressed her palms to his chest. "Thank you," she said, her soft voice brushing warmly against his ear.

Tinjin wrapped his arms around her. "You're welcome," he whispered back as he relished the feel of her.

He placed a gentle kiss against her cheek, allowing his lips to linger there for a minute longer than necessary. Her breathing eased as she relaxed against him. He dropped his cheek to her cheek, the warmth of her skin sending a swift chill down his spine.

Natalie slid her arms around his torso and hugged her chest to his. He wrapped his arms around her back, his hands resting against the silk of her dress. She fit nicely in his arms, her body melding beautifully with his own as they embraced. Letting her go was the last thing on his mind until he looked up and noticed their siblings eyeing them both intently.

Chapter 7

"I thought you were engaged to some business tycoon?" Naomi asked. She shifted her body against the queen-size mattress in their brother's guest room. The two women had spent the night with their brother, still recovering from their mother's funeral.

"Where'd you get that idea?" Natalie questioned.

"You were in a picture with him in *Forbes* magazine. It said you were his fiancée. Norris-Jean saved a copy of it. His name was Paul or John or something like that."

Natalie rolled her eyes. "Jean-Paul Vivier is only a friend. We are not engaged and never have been."

"Are you sure about that? Because he looked engaged. And, if I recall, that was a serious diamond you were sporting on your left hand. Eighteen carats, I think."

Natalie laughed. "Let's just say he was generous with his gifts."

"Uh-huh…generous…I hear ya!" Naomi exclaimed as she laughed with her sister. "So tell me more about Tinjin. You two seem pretty cozy for having just met."

"Being stuck together in an airport will make you cozy. But I like him."

"So is this just a fling? A little one-night-stand kind of thing? Because that might be awkward at any future family events with our new cousins."

Natalie shook her head. "I don't know what it is, so we're going to have to wait and see. I just think he's a nice guy and I haven't met a whole lot of nice guys."

"I'm thinking if your boyfriends are so generous with gifts then you must be all kinds of nice, too."

Natalie shrugged. "Jean-Paul likes to buy his relationships. I wasn't interested in being bought. Money isn't everything."

Naomi's eyes widened. "Well, that's refreshing to hear! Before you left you would have sworn that money *was* everything."

"That's because we didn't have any."

Naomi shook her head. "I think we all felt that way at one point or another. But we're doing well now."

"Are you happy, Naomi?" Natalie asked. She

dropped her body down on the bed beside her sister, crossing her long limbs beneath her.

The two women sat staring at each other as Naomi pondered the question. She finally nodded. "I am happy. Things are really going well. My business is growing. The boys are all doing well and my baby sister is home. So, yeah, I'm very happy."

"Was Norris-Jean happy?"

"Our mother was as happy as she could ever be. I think *content* would be a better word to describe what Norris-Jean felt."

"I feel so guilty. I should have…"

"Don't," Naomi snapped, cutting off her comment. "You did exactly what you were supposed to do. Noah stayed to take care of her, and Norris-Jean resented that more than anything else. He won't admit it but it hurt his feelings. She loved us but she wanted us to go and do better. She was happy when we left. She loved being able to brag about everything her children had accomplished. She bragged about you a lot. So don't you dare start throwing yourself a pity party! That's not how our mother raised us. Honor her death by moving on and moving forward."

"Life is about living your dreams," Natalie said softly, quoting the words they'd heard the matriarch say over and over again growing up.

"A few years ago Norris-Jean cut a quote out of some magazine she'd been reading. I couldn't tell you the author but it read, 'Life is not meant to be lived such that we cross over well-groomed and attractive, but rather that we slide in sideways, champagne in one hand, strawberries in the other, clothes in tatters, our bodies completely worn and totally spent, shouting, *WOOHOO! What a ride!'* After that she used to say, 'live the ride.' That's what she wanted for all of us. We owe her that."

Natalie smiled as she leaned to give her sister a warm hug. The two women held onto each other tightly. Both swiped tears from their eyes when they finally broke the embrace.

"Are you and Tinjin spending the whole day together? Because the city's really not that big," Naomi questioned, changing the subject.

Natalie laughed. "I just thought it would be nice to show him some of the tourist sites."

"So where are you two going for breakfast?" Naomi asked. She glanced down to her wristwatch.

Natalie's grin widened. "I don't know yet. But I'm thinking champagne and strawberries would be a nice place to start."

Tinjin was seated in the hotel lobby when Natalie stepped inside. He couldn't help but notice the attention she garnered as she came to a stop and struck a pose as she looked about. She was stunning, looking every bit the high-profile fashion model that she was.

She was dressed in a long-sleeved white crop top featuring a crew neckline, spandex fabric at the front and a sheer textured fabric at the back. She'd paired it with a matching pencil skirt, its perfect fit an essential in every woman's closet. The skirt was high waisted with a slit at the back and it complemented her lean frame. Five-inch black platform high heels with signature red bottoms were her shoe of choice and she carried a red Hermès Birkin bag.

He rose from his seat and eased his way over to her side, surprising her as she stared in the opposite direction. Natalie jumped, startled by his touch as he slid an arm around her waist and leaned to kiss her cheek.

"Good morning," he said, his warm breath blowing against her skin.

"Hey!" Natalie responded, her face flushing with color. "You scared me!"

"I didn't mean to," he said with a soft smile.

Natalie smiled back. "So what would you like to do today?"

He shrugged. "Whatever you'd like. I'm riding shotgun."

She smirked, the pull to her face lifting her eyes brightly. "I hate driving."

Tinjin shrugged. "Oh, well."

"I'm better at giving directions," she persisted.

He laughed. "I'm on vacation and this is your stomping ground," he countered.

She narrowed her gaze as it swept over his face. Amusement danced with the bright light that flickered in her eyes. Tinjin resisted the urge to fall headfirst and lose himself in the stare she was giving him. He changed the subject.

"I love the outfit. Who's the designer?"

"Vivian Chan."

"Beautiful," he said as he took her hand and gave her a slight spin.

"I'm impressed, as well," she said as her gaze ran the length of his body. His slacks and blazer were a deep charcoal gray over a dark gray silk T-shirt that he'd partnered with casual black suede loafers. He was polished and well put together. And he had the brightest, most endearing smile.

"We both know how to dress and dress well," Tinjin said. "That's a good sign. It shows we're compatible."

Natalie laughed. "And vain."

Tinjin chuckled with her. "Very vain. But it's a necessary vice in our business."

Nodding in agreement, Natalie slipped her arm through his. "Come on," she said. "Let's go play tourist."

Hours later Natalie and Tinjin were laughing heartily as they waited for their first meal of the day to be delivered to their table. Natalie had spent the morning driving them around as she'd reminisced about her days growing up in the city. She'd driven him past her former high school, the church she'd been raised in, the small building that had housed her first job. Then there'd been those places she'd been unable to frequent, the ones that had been too pricey or simply inaccessible to a girl who'd been raised on her side of town. Places she could now buy and sell without blinking an eye. The memories had been bittersweet as she'd pretended to not be fazed, trying to keep the emotion from her eyes. But Tinjin had not missed the lingering looks that had spoken volumes when she'd drifted off into reflection.

She'd eventually chosen the Copper Onion for their midday meal, an upscale eatery that boasted a gourmet menu sourced from local farmers and purveyors. Tinjin had selected the wine, a chenin blanc blend that paired nicely with the steak salad that he'd ordered and the portobello-and-white-mushroom risotto she'd chosen. Natalie savored the first sip as she stared at him.

"Nice selection," she said as she palmed her glass between her hands. "Very nice."

"Thank you." He looked around the room. "So how long has this place been here?"

Natalie shook her head. "I don't know. This whole area was dirt and dust when I left. I can't believe all the changes since I've been gone."

Tinjin chuckled as a wave of sadness flushed her cheeks. "Don't feel bad. It's just a sign of the times. You could come back in two weeks and something else would be different. Unless you're standing still there's no way you can keep up with things changing!"

"I guess you have a point," Natalie said.

There was a brief lull in the conversation as the waitress came to a stop at the table, hot plates juggled precariously in her arms. When their meals were settled in front of them and the waitress moved on to another table, Tinjin bowed his head in prayer. Natalie watched as he whispered a word of thanks and gratitude. When he lifted his head, his gaze resting on her face, she felt herself blush, heat warming her cheeks.

"You don't bless your food?" Tinjin questioned as he took his first bite.

She smiled. "I do, but it's been a while since I've seen any man do it. Not a whole lot of black Baptist churches and congregations in London."

"Baptists aren't the only ones who pray, Gnat."

"You know what I mean."

He smiled back. "I do. It took me a while to get used to the European aesthetic, as well."

"It's definitely not Salt Lake City. I like London, though. I like everything about it."

"I like London, too. But I love Paris."

"Do you speak French?"

"Je parle français et plusieurs autres langues couramment."

"And several other languages fluently," she echoed. "I'm impressed, TJ."

"You should be."

"And your several other languages include...?"

"Ich spreche deutsch. Yo hablo español. Parlo

italiano." He shrugged nonchalantly. "And I speak just a smidgen of Japanese," he said.

"You're quite the Renaissance man, aren't you?"

"Girl, I'm the new breed of alpha male. I'm the whole enchilada, the bag of chips *and* I'm in touch with my sensitive side." Tinjin dusted off his left shoulder with the backs of his fingers.

Natalie laughed. "You're full of yourself, too!"

"Much like you, beautiful lady, I have my moments." He met the look she was giving him, laughter shimmering in his eyes.

Tinjin's smile was captivating, the depths of it brightening his face. His eyes were dazzling, seeming to illuminate the entire room. Natalie found herself relishing the warmth he exuded, everything about the man feeling like comfort food and home.

The rest of the afternoon was a blur as they hit all the tourist spots, snapping an endless stream of cell phone selfies to commemorate their time together. Tinjin couldn't remember the last time he'd laughed so hard or as much. Natalie was great company. She had a quirky, dry sense of humor and her quick wit kept him on his toes. Together they played off each other like two dance partners who'd been performing together for years. It was the most natural give-and-take of any relationship he'd ever had and they were far from being in a relationship. But they were quickly becoming fast friends and Tinjin liked the dynamics growing between them.

"How long are you staying in Salt Lake City?"

he asked as he savored the last bite of his late-night dessert, a crème brûlée from a little coffee shop in the downtown area.

"I'll probably head back to London at the end of the week. My brother has to be in Los Angeles for a game on Sunday so he and Nathaniel both are leaving Friday. And Naomi is heading back to Arizona on Saturday. What about you? Where are you headed next?"

"Dallas. I want to spend time with my grandmother and a few more days with my sister and her family before I go back to London."

"How long will you be in London before you move to Paris?"

"Just a few weeks. I have some meetings set up about my business and once I've finished those I'll need to get right to work."

Natalie nodded. "If you can squeeze it into your schedule I would love to cook dinner for you when you get back to London."

"You can cook?" he questioned, one eyebrow raised.

She stared at him. "I'm a very good cook," she snapped, her tone curt.

Tinjin laughed. "Why'd you say it like that? I just asked the question!"

"You were trying to be funny, TJ, but you're not. You're not funny at all!"

He shrugged. "I wasn't trying to be funny. I just asked if you could cook because you don't look like the type of woman who'd know her way around a stove."

"What kind of woman do I look like?" Natalie said, her body tensing with rising annoyance.

Tinjin grinned, his smile wide and teasing. He gave her a deep stare but said nothing, ignoring her question. "So what do you cook that's good?"

"Everything I cook is good. I'll have you know that I'm a master around the stove," she answered, her eyes becoming thin slits.

Tinjin nodded. "I believe you."

There was a moment of pause as Natalie gave him a harsh look, exasperation painting her expression.

"I do," he repeated. "I really do. I'm sure you're a superior cook and everything you touch tastes like heaven."

Natalie pursed her lips tightly, a full pout pulling at her mouth. "Now you have jokes."

Tinjin laughed. "Don't get your knickers twisted. I was just teasing," he said with a soft chuckle.

Natalie rolled her eyes. "I'm leaving. Find your own way home," she said as she stood up abruptly. She put her cloth napkin on the table and grabbed her purse. "And don't call me!"

Wide-eyed, Tinjin watched her as she stomped toward the front door. He called after her. "Natalie, wait!" He placed cash onto the table to cover the tab, then rushed behind her, grabbing at her elbow just as she stepped out the door. "Really, I was just kidding!" he said as he spun her toward him.

Natalie laughed, merriment shimmering in her eyes. "So was I," she said. "But I like how you came after me. I liked that a lot."

"You play too much!" Tinjin exclaimed. The look across his face wafted between annoyance and amusement.

"Only when I have someone to play with," she responded nonchalantly.

"Well, I'm not interested in your games."

Natalie smiled, her gaze teasing. "Yes, you are," she said as she took a step toward him, brushing her palms across the front of his shirt.

Tinjin grinned back, his own stare sweeping across her face. "Yes, I am."

The two stood eyeing each other, the heat between them rising with a vengeance. Natalie gasped when Tinjin suddenly reached his arm around her waist and pulled her to him. She settled against the rising hardness of his taut muscles, her soft curves caving nicely against him. Their gazes were still locked one to the other, eyes dancing back and forth. Natalie's mouth was parted slightly and when she snaked her tongue past her lips, licking them lightly, Tinjin tightened the hold he had around her torso.

He pulled her even closer and with no hesitation dropped his mouth to hers. His lips skated against her lips easily, the plush pillows gliding like silk against silk. They both tasted sweet, like the dessert they'd just consumed, and there was the faintest hint of mocha cappuccino on her breath. He inhaled the scent of her, a deep influx of air that filled his lungs and nourished his spirit. He kissed her and it felt like the first kiss he'd ever had, every nerve ending in his body surging with delight. The pleasure was intoxicating and he suddenly felt addicted, unable to fathom ever having enough of her.

Natalie kissed him back. She kissed him with every fiber of her body, every sinew melting against him. She felt safe and secure in his arms and the delightful sensations sweeping through her were intense. Nothing compared to the brilliance of the moment, everything seeming to fall into place when she'd least expected it. His hands tapped gently down her spine, his fingertips igniting a wave of combustion that emanated from her feminine spirit. She felt as if she'd been dropped straight into heaven and nothing could pull her from the moment.

Saying goodbye was proving to be more problematic than Tinjin would ever have imagined. Natalie had driven him to the airport and now they stood together in the American Airlines ticket area, wrapped around each other. Their kisses were even sweeter than the night before and Tinjin realized just how much he was going to miss having her around.

"Call me when you land in Dallas," Natalie said, pressing her cheek to his.

"I will." Tinjin dropped his eyes down to stare at her. "And you owe me dinner when we get back to London."

Natalie laughed. "You lost your chance at any free meal I cook," she said.

He shrugged his shoulders. "Then get someone else to cook it, but it better be as good as you claim your cooking is." His smile was haughty as he kissed her one last time. He winked, then turned and headed off toward the security line.

Natalie watched him walk away, staring until he waved one last time and disappeared from view. She suddenly felt empty and anxious for time to pass so that she could see him again. The new emotion was awkward and disconcerting, something she'd never felt before. She took a deep breath and then a second, once again fighting back tears.

Her cell phone suddenly rang, a new text message registering on the device. Depressing the buttons, she read the greeting once and then a second time. *I miss you already.* Her smile was miles wide. Her new friend TJ had just made her entire day.

Chapter 8

Pulling into the driveway of his grandmother's home lifted Tinjin's spirits until he felt as though he might actually burst with sheer joy. Coming home always had that effect on him. The small cottage was a welcome sight, with its bright arrangements of flora that decorated the landscape. His grandmother's gardens were the pride of the neighborhood and the saltbox architecture gleamed with light and warmth.

As Tinjin sat in the driveway, his rental car idling in Park, everything about the homestead reminded him of all that was good about growing up beneath the watchful eye of Deloriann Braddy. He and his sister had both been blessed to have the matriarch to depend on. After both of his parents had disappeared from his life he had never taken his grandmother's love for granted, and he and Tierra both were mindful to show their appreciation every chance they could.

Mama Dee was standing at the kitchen sink when he entered the home using the key he'd had possession of since he was a young boy. She was a robust woman dressed in her usual inside attire, a cotton housecoat and satin bedroom slippers. From her large eyes and full cheeks down to her thick legs and wide ankles, everything about her was round in a pleasant, soft-dough kind of way.

Her largesse filled the room with personality. The warmth she exuded was almost contrary to the stainless-steel appliances and rich ebony color of the granite countertops. Mama Dee was more like the exterior of her home, with its brightly painted shutters, sweeping porches and massive floral beds, each conflicting with its redecorated interior. As he stood in the entranceway staring, Tinjin almost regretted his and Tierra's decision to gut the home's insides to give their grandmother new bathrooms and a chef's kitchen.

The older woman's gregarious voice boomed warmly. "How you gone just come into my house and not speak!"

Tinjin grinned. "Hey, Mama Dee! I just got a little sentimental. It feels good to be home."

Her own bright smile warmed Tinjin's heart as Mama Dee extended her arms in her grandson's direction. "Come give me some suga', boy!"

Stepping into her outstretched arms, Tinjin hugged and kissed the matriarch, reminded of those moments he'd felt safe and secure in her embrace. Wrapped in his grandmother's love, Tinjin let a tear drip from his eyes, swiping it away before she noticed.

"So how long you plan on being home?" she asked, gesturing for him to take a seat at her kitchen table.

"For a few days if you'll have me."

Mama Dee nodded. "Son, you know this will always be your home. You don't need to ask to stay. I'll be glad for the company. Was just about to work the gardens and I could use the help. My knees aren't as good as they use to be."

Tinjin chuckled. "Why don't I change my clothes and then we'll see what I can help you with."

"I was just about to get my midday coffee and a chicken salad sandwich first. Are you hungry?"

"Is that your famous chicken salad?"

"You know I don't eat nobody else's so I don't know why you asking that foolishness!"

He nodded. "I would love something to eat. I've missed your cooking."

Mama Dee winked as she moved to the refrigerator, pulling a Tupperware container from inside. Just as Tinjin started to take a seat at the kitchen table his grandmother admonished him to go wash his hands. He felt like he was ten years old again and it made him smile. By the time he returned to the kitchen the table was set with two sandwiches on her favorite porcelain plates, a side salad and two steaming cups of rich, black coffee. When he was settled in his seat, Mama Dee blessed the food, offering up a prayer of thanksgiving.

"How was your flight?" Mama Dee asked as they both took their first bites of the afternoon meal.

Tinjin swiped at the crumbs that dusted his lips with a paper napkin before answering. "It was good. I got stuck in New York coming from London. They had some major snow that slowed us down."

Mama Dee's head bobbed against her thick neck. "I spoke to your sister. She tells me you met a woman while you were stuck there at that airport."

Tinjin laughed. "I'm sure Tierra had a lot to say."

"She did."

"Well, it's nothing for you or Tierra to concern yourselves with. Natalie and I are just friends."

Tinjin could feel his grandmother's intense stare boring into him. He focused on his sandwich, refusing to meet the look he knew she was giving him.

"Just friends?"

Tinjin nodded as he drew a forkful of salad into his mouth.

"You don't need to be rushing into any relationship with that girl, Tinjin. That baby just lost her mother. She needs some time to work through that. She don't need to be starting no new relationships right now."

Tinjin gave his grandmother a quick look. "We're not rushing into anything."

The old woman's gaze narrowed.

"Really, Mama Dee! We're not!"

"Mind what I tell you," she said. "I've lived longer and I know more."

Tinjin laughed. "Yes, ma'am."

Both finished their meal. The conversation was casual as they caught up with each other. Then his grandmother made plans for his time.

"You should change your clothes now so you can come help me out in the gardens. Tomorrow I expect you to come to bible study with me at the church. Congregation ain't seen you in a good while. Be nice for you to catch up with everyone since you won't be here for Sunday service."

"Yes, Mama Dee."

Tinjin's cell phone suddenly vibrated. As he read the text message on the screen his smile widened into a full grin. He and Natalie had been communicating back and forth since he'd left Salt Lake City. Her humor was contagious, each of her messages moving him to laughter.

His grandmother eyed him curiously as his thumbs danced over the screen, texting back. The reply made him smile even wider. The back-and-forth went on for a good five minutes before Tinjin realized he'd gotten distracted. "Sorry," he said, a sheepish expression washing over his face.

Mama Dee shook her head. "Lord, have mercy!"

she exclaimed as she moved onto her feet, beginning to clear away the dirty dishes.

"What, Mama Dee?"

"You not only rushed into it, but you so far gone I wouldn't be surprised if you two already planning the wedding."

Tinjin's laugh was gut deep. "No one's planning any wedding, Mama Dee."

"Uh-huh!"

"You worry too much."

His grandmother laughed. "I'm not worried about a thing. But don't think I don't know you, Tinjin. I raised you and I can see it all over your face. That girl has your nose wide open! So you better make sure I meet this girl soon."

Tinjin grinned, his head moving from side to side. "Yes, ma'am!"

"You're glowing! You're not pregnant, are you?"

Natalie laughed as her best friend and partner in crime, Frenchie Adams, eyed her suspiciously. Frenchie had been the first person Natalie had met when she'd first arrived in London. Just a few years older, the expat had been working as a graphic designer for a small clothing firm, creating the designs for the fashion house's seasonal look books. The two women had bumped into each other as Natalie had stood outside a corner bakery, counting the last of her change in hopes she'd be able to buy herself a croissant. Recognizing the hunger in her eyes, Frenchie had taken Natalie under her wing, giving her a blanket and her living-room couch to rest her head on and enough food to squash the pangs of hunger that rippled through her abdomen. Frenchie had been her first connection to the fashion industry, pointing her in all the right directions. The rest was history and both knew beyond a shadow of a doubt that they would remain friends forever.

"I'm serious. Something's changed," Frenchie persisted.

"Well, I'm definitely not pregnant," Natalie said.

The two women sat in a corner booth at one of their favorite eateries, Seven Park Place at the St. James's hotel. Frenchie's dark eyes narrowed with suspicion.

"Then it has to be a man!" she suddenly exclaimed, excitement billowing with her words. "A rich man!"

"Why does he have to be rich?"

Frenchie tossed her a look. "He doesn't have to be," she said, her facial expression contradicting her comment. "But it would be nice."

Natalie laughed, shaking her head.

"I'm just saying," Frenchie quipped. "You disappear for two weeks for your mama's funeral and come back like you just won the lottery. Something's amiss, my friend."

Natalie's eyes rolled a second time. She took a deep breath. "My brother Noah says the mourning will probably hit me in a few weeks." She shrugged.

"Right now, though, I just feel…I don't know…relieved? It's like going home took a heavy burden off my shoulders."

"You reconnected with your family. And family that you didn't even know you had. That was a nice reminder that you're not alone."

Natalie nodded.

"But that still doesn't explain that gleam in your eyes," Frenchie said.

"I did meet someone and I think he's a really nice guy," Natalie said.

Frenchie snapped her fingers. She bounced up and down in her seat. "I knew it! Girl, a good man will do it to you every time!"

"He's a designer and he currently lives in London, but is moving to Paris."

"You could live in Paris. I could see that."

Natalie took a deep breath. "Our two families are actually connected in the United States. His sister is married to my cousin."

"So he comes with trustworthy references. When do I get to meet him?"

"He's flying back tonight. Hopefully I'll be able to see him tomorrow, or maybe the day after. I don't know when you'll meet him!"

"Girl, you better meet that man at the airport! We can go together. Welcome him home proper!"

"I can't just show up at the airport."

"Why not?"

"I'd look desperate and I don't want to seem overly eager," she stated.

Frenchie laughed. "But you are desperate."

Natalie laughed with her. "Maybe I am but he doesn't need to know that."

"What have I told you about playing games with men?"

"I'm not playing games

"Keep telling yourself that."

"I'm not playing games, but I do intend to keep him on his toes."

"So what's his name?"

"Tinjin. Tinjin Braddy."

Frenchie's eyes narrowed slightly. "Interesting."

Natalie smiled. "It's different."

"So what about Jean-Paul?" Frenchie suddenly questioned. Curiosity furrowed her brow.

Natalie met her friend's deep stare. She hadn't given the notorious Jean-Paul Vivier a single thought in weeks. The billionaire playboy was someone she'd dated briefly, his interest in her far more serious than hers had ever been. He'd wined and dined her, had lavished her with gifts and had been overwhelmingly annoying.

That, and there was something about his lack of personal hygiene that was repulsive. His mouth was a disaster area, teeth twisted, one or two missing, and the coloration, a garish shade of yellow, was off-putting to the point of distraction.

His referring to her as his fiancée at the last social event they'd attended together had been the final straw. Marrying Jean-Paul was not on her personal radar, the man coming nowhere close to being a man she could see herself doing forever with. She'd begun to push him away, refusing to take his calls and ignoring him publicly. Her efforts had only served to further fuel his interest.

She shrugged dismissively. "What about him?"

Her friend's expression was teasing as she crossed her arms over her chest. "So, it's like that now?"

"It's been like that for a while and you know it. I am not interested in Jean-Paul."

"I don't think Jean-Paul is ready to be dismissed like that."

Natalie shrugged again, her eyes rolling. "That's his problem. Not mine. Besides, I know for a fact he attended the Met Gala in New York with some new hip-hop artist. Jean-Paul has moved on just like he should have."

"He didn't go with her. They were just photographed together."

"Whatever. It's not my concern."

Frenchie sat staring at her for a brief moment.

"What?"

"Nothing."

"I didn't think so," Natalie quipped and the two women laughed heartily.

They continued to catch up with each other, their conversation peppered with one-liners and laughter. The discourse was comfortable and Natalie felt at ease with her best friend. She was excited to catch her up on the details of her meeting Tinjin and as she shared the experience, she found herself grinning from ear to ear, the memories like the sweetest balm across her spirit.

Hours later Natalie was still riding the clouds of a very happy high. She stole a quick glance toward her clock radio as she slipped between her bedsheets. She reached for her cell phone and dialed Tinjin, his number programmed on her speed dial. The phone rang twice and then a third time before Tinjin answered, breathing heavily into the receiver.

"So what were you doing?" Natalie questioned. She pulled her knees to her chest as she settled her back against the bed pillows.

"I was cutting grass," Tinjin said. "With a push mower and it is exceptionally hot here in Texas."

Natalie smiled. "Awww! How sweet you are, helping out your grandmother."

"I don't know about all that. I know I wasn't expecting to work quite this hard on vacation," he said with a wry laugh.

"Well, I like your grandmother and I enjoyed talking to her on the phone the other day. I can't wait to meet her."

"Mama Dee can't wait to meet you, too. So, what are you doing?"

"Headed to bed. I have a long day tomorrow."

"That sounds interesting."

"It really isn't. I'll be running errands in the morning and then I have a photo shoot in the afternoon."

Tinjin nodded. "My plane leaves at seven tonight. Barring any bad weather in New York, my international connection should leave just before midnight and put me in London sometime before nine o'clock in the morning."

"Well, let's hope you don't get snowed in."

"I'm keeping my fingers crossed," Tinjin said. There was a moment's hesitation as he listened to her breathing on the other end. Her breath was a soft inhale and exhalation, her calm energy wafting through the receiver. "So, you're cooking dinner for me tomorrow night, right?" Tinjin asked.

Natalie laughed, the wealth of it like a sweet jingle against Tinjin's ear.

He smiled widely. "Why are you laughing? I'm being serious."

"I told you I was not cooking for you ever. That train has pulled out of the station."

Tinjin laughed this time. "You never said you were never ever going to cook for me."

"I know what I said. You just heard what you wanted to hear."

"Oh, I know what I heard. I heard you promise me a home-cooked meal when we were both back home. Tomorrow we will both be back in London. Besides, you can't stay mad at me and you know it. I'm too damn cute."

"You are so full of yourself!"

"I am but I'm not a picky eater so anything you cook should be fine. As long as it's good and since you were bragging about how good you are I'm sure whatever you fix will be fine."

"You done?" Natalie asked.

"Don't forget dessert," Tinjin added. "I have a weakness for anything sweet and chocolate is, of course, my absolute favorite."

"You're unbelievable!" Natalie gushed.

"Not really," Tinjin said. He could feel her smiling and he imagined the amusement that painted her expression. "What are you wearing?" His voice dropped two octaves as his question rang between them.

Natalie's eyes widened slightly. "Excuse me?" She stole a quick glance down to the flannel pajamas she wore. "You did not just ask me that!"

Tinjin's imagination was roused as he pondered the possibility. "So, you're wearing nothing. Is it nothing like panties-and-a-bra nothing or nothing like naked-as-the-day-you-were-born nothing? Do you go commando when you sleep?"

"Nothing like it's none of your business nothing," she responded with a soft giggle.

"So, nothing like you're only wearing moisturizer and body spray." Tinjin hummed softly. "Hmmm! That sounds enticing."

"Goodbye, TJ," Natalie said, grateful that he couldn't see the soft blush that had risen to her cheeks. "Have a safe flight."

"Good night, Gnat. I can't wait to see you to-morrow."

There was no hesitation as Natalie responded. "I feel the same way!"

Chapter 9

They were a small crowd standing in a half circle with balloons and signs that bore his name and welcomed him home. Natalie led the group of five women, her sign bigger than the others, her smile the widest. They erupted in a loud cheer as he stepped past the doors of the luggage area at Heathrow airport, looking for a taxi to carry him home.

Tinjin smiled as he looked from one eager face to the next, curious to know who they all were. Slightly embarrassed by all the hoopla, he stole a quick glance over one shoulder and then the other, mindful of all the travelers who were eyeing them curiously. As he approached, Natalie stepped toward him, easing her body against his. She lifted her face upward, her lips pursed and trembling with excitement as they met his. He looped his arms around her waist and pulled her even closer as he kissed her back, his own excitement tightening every muscle in his body.

"Welcome home," Natalie whispered when they finally broke the connection.

"Yeah, welcome home," Frenchie said as she pushed her way between them. Her hand was extended in greeting. "Hi, it's very nice to meet you!"

Tinjin laughed heartily. "It's nice to meet you, too! Who are you?"

Natalie laughed with him. "Tinjin, this is my best friend, Frenchie. And that's Catherine, Leslie and Imani."

The other women all waved, greeting him warmly.

"This is quite a surprise," Tinjin said as he gave Natalie a quick squeeze.

"I figured I'd bring the whole cheerleading team to welcome you home. Plus, I figured you might need a ride."

His grin was warm and bright. "I could get used to this," he said.

Frenchie laughed. "Don't get too used to it. We need to get to work," she said as she stole a quick glance down to her wristwatch. "Hopefully we'll be able to see you again sometime soon, Mr. Braddy!"

"I look forward to it," he answered. "And please, call me Tinjin!"

"You hear that, right, Natalie? Tinjin looks forward to seeing us again so make sure that happens."

Tinjin laughed.

Natalie rolled her eyes. She leaned to kiss her friend's cheek. "Go to work, please!"

The other three women all moved to give her a hug. "We're doing drinks after work," Imani said, her Cockney accent thick and heavy. "It'll be the perfect opportunity for us to get to know you better." She gave Tinjin a wink as she kissed her friend.

Tinjin tossed Natalie a quick look. She scowled, her eyes rolling skyward. The other women all laughed.

"Don't get your brassiere twisted," the woman named Catherine said with a soft giggle. "She was just teasing!"

"No, she wasn't," Natalie said, her lip snarling slightly. She fanned her friends away. "Thank you, ladies. Now, goodbye."

She and Tinjin watched as Frenchie and the rest of her crew disappeared into the parking garage, all of them still laughing heartily.

"So, would you like a ride?" Natalie asked, turning her attention back to Tinjin.

"I would," he said, but first you need to welcome me home properly," he said.

"I beg your pardon?"

"You heard me," Tinjin teased.

She giggled softly as he pulled her back to him and kissed her again. Natalie gasped and as she inhaled the scent of him a wave of heat spiraled deep into her core. His tongue teased her lips, then snaked past the line of her teeth to dance inside the warm lining of her mouth. The moment was intoxicating, leaving them both breathing heavily when he finally pulled himself from her, loosening the hold he had around her body.

Her eyes were wide and she panted softly. "So how was that for a welcome home?" she finally managed to ask.

Tinjin nodded. "That…" He paused to catch his breath. "That was good!"

Tinjin's West End home was quaint and casual, befitting his easygoing demeanor. The decor was purposely sparse against bright white walls and oversize windows. A red-and-gold-striped settee and black leather sectional sat in a far corner with an oversize black lacquer table anchoring them. A rustic dining table surrounded by upholstered leather and tweed fabric chairs took up significant space, the table's surface stacked with paper and pencil drawings. At a glance nothing went together but somehow Tinjin's accessorizing had made it work, the elegant styling like a vision out of a magazine.

"Impressive," Natalie said as she walked the interior, eyeing his personal possessions. She moved to the window to peer out to the landscape.

"It's comfortable."

She nodded as she turned to face him. "It does feel homey. I really like it. I might need you to give me a few suggestions. My place is very museumlike."

"A little cold and stiff?" Tinjin quipped. "Like you?"

Her eyes widened. "I am not cold or stiff, thank you very much!"

Tinjin laughed as he moved to her side, pulling her into his arms. "I know you aren't. I was just teasing." He blew a soft sigh as he dropped his face into the length of her hair. He took a deep breath, inhaling the scent of mango and shea butter that nourished her hair. "So, what's on your agenda today?"

Rising onto her toes Natalie kissed his cheek before pulling herself from his arms. Heat had risen with a vengeance and she needed to put some serious space between them. Tinjin eyed her, a coy smile pulling at his full lips. His muscles had tightened and he understood the sudden need for a cool breeze to blow between them. She moved to the settee and sat down, pulling a pillow to her chest.

"I have a photo shoot in an hour and then I'm headed home to cook dinner. I have company coming. What about you? Anything planned for this afternoon?"

"I have a meeting in a few hours," he said as he glanced at his watch. "Then I'm coming to your house to get my dinner...and my dessert." His smile was smug as he met her gaze.

Natalie laughed. "I don't remember anyone promising you dessert."

"Can't have dinner without having dessert."

"Says you."

"Says everybody."

She laughed again as she moved back onto her feet and headed in the direction of the door. "I don't put much stock in what everybody has to say," she retorted.

Tinjin moved behind her, his strides long and quick. He reached the door just as she grasped for the handle. He kicked the luggage he'd rested there earlier out of his way. He stretched an arm around her waist and cradled her against himself, the curve of her buttocks sinking nicely along the bulge through his groin. Then he planted a damp kiss at the back of her neck.

Natalie gasped, gyrating her hips back against him. "You don't play fair," she muttered, fighting to stall the waves of heat that had suddenly flooded her body.

"Neither do you," Tinjin murmured as he continued to nibble at her flesh, the length of an erection hardening against her backside.

Natalie suddenly pushed him from her. She took a long inhale, then let the warm breath out slowly. Spinning in his arms she kissed him one last time, her sensuous touch eager and yearning.

"Don't be late, TJ! I'd hate to see someone else get your sweets," she said teasingly. Then she spun on her heel and out the door, the memory of her touch still burning hot against Tinjin's lips.

Tinjin sighed again as he closed the door behind her, pressing his forehead to the wooden structure.

His body quivered slightly as he sucked in deep breaths to steady his nerves.

He liked Natalie. He liked her a lot. Her impromptu welcoming party at the airport had been an enlightening moment. He'd been missing her and until that moment hadn't realized just how much. Everything about the beauty excited him. She was quickly becoming his drug of choice and it was becoming harder to deny his addiction. But he knew that Natalie Stallion was a woman who was going to make him work for whatever happened between them. And she was going to make him work hard. Standing there thinking about her, with the lengthy protrusion in his slacks tight and hard, Tinjin knew beyond any doubts that he'd be willing to do whatever it took to have her.

Natalie was still shaking as she made her way to her car. She could still feel Tinjin's hands and fingers, the warmth from them having ignited every one of her nerve endings. The fervor was explosive and she was grateful for the cool rain that had begun to fall overhead. The moisture was just enough to stall the tremors of heat that had threatened to consume her.

She took a deep breath and then a second.

Her desire for Tinjin Braddy was mystifying, like nothing she'd ever experienced before. Seeing him again had ignited something torrid inside her and she felt herself falling headfirst into the growing emotion that swept between them like a firestorm. She had needed to put some serious distance between them, to soothe the desire and urgency that had risen with a vengeance with his touch. Natalie knew that if she had stayed, nothing would have stopped her from giving in to the yearning that had threatened to expose itself.

She inhaled swiftly, filling her lungs with the cool morning air. She was excited about the prospect of what might happen with her and Tinjin. So much so that she couldn't think straight and Natalie had never before felt so out of control with any man.

Pulling her car into traffic she trembled with anticipation. Thoughts of Tinjin spiraled through her head as she pondered the possibilities. She suddenly smiled. Dinner might have to wait. Dessert suddenly had her full attention.

Chapter 10

Jean-Paul Vivier extended his hand in greeting. Tinjin smiled and shook it eagerly.

"It's nice to finally meet you," Jean-Paul said, his thick accent sounding like his tongue was wrapped in sandpaper. "Your reputation precedes you."

"Thank you," Tinjin said as Jean-Paul gestured toward an empty leather seat in his office. "It's nice to meet you, as well, and I appreciate you taking this meeting with me."

"Well, I was very excited when I heard you were looking for an investor. I have been a big fan of your men's line for years and I am quite impressed with the strides you've made with all your other endeavors. Your designs are stellar and you've made quite a name for yourself. Everyone in the industry is talking about you and that's the kind of partner I'd like to have."

Tinjin nodded. "Well, I appreciate the kind words, but as I told you on the phone, I'm not looking for a hands-on partner. I'm looking for venture capital, a line of credit that will allow me to grow my business without any financial distractions."

Jean-Paul nodded, his dark eyes locked squarely on Tinjin's face. He leaned back in his leather executive's chair, one hand caressing the short length of goatee that adorned his broad chin. "I reviewed your prospectus and as it stands now, if I invest, I'd be taking all the risk. So why should I gamble my money on you?"

Tinjin leaned back in his seat, as well, crossing his ankle over his knee. He clasped both hands around his calf, clutching his lower leg. "Because I'm exceptionally good at what I do," he started as he proceeded to support that statement with facts and data. His numbers were impressive as he quantified his accomplishments in the numeric language venture capitalists thrived on. "In return," he concluded, "you'll get your investment back with interest, as well as a two-and-one-half percent share of my company."

Jean-Paul nodded slowly. "I couldn't even consider this deal for less than ten percent."

"Everything's negotiable but if I consider a larger percentage of the equity, then I would expect a significantly lower interest rate, like three percent instead of thirty."

The other man smiled, the lift to his lips showcasing an imperfect grille. It was a stark contrast with his expensive silk suit, manicured eyebrows and Elvis Presley haircut.

"I'm throwing a dinner party in a few weeks, after I get back from Italy. My assistant will call you with the details. Plan to attend," Jean-Paul said. "I'll have my answer for you then."

Tinjin rose to his feet. He extended his hand. "It was a pleasure to meet you, Mr. Vivier," he said before heading toward the door.

As the door closed and locked after Tinjin's exit, Jean-Paul reached for his cell phone and depressed a speed dial number. He held the device gingerly as he waited for someone on the other end to answer. Seconds later, when the call was forwarded to voice mail, he left a message. "Natalia, darling! It's me, Jean-Paul. I'm having a small gathering of industry powerhouses. It wouldn't be a party if you weren't there. I also hear the Chanel group is looking for a new face. I've already plugged you for the job so you really need to show up so I can introduce you to Karl Lagerfeld. I'll call you back with all the details."

Natalie deleted the messages on her answering machine, only bothering to make a mental note to return her agent's call. The others could call her back,

or not, she thought as she moved into her bedroom
to change her clothes.

Dinner was simmering nicely in the oven and she
had just enough time to take a quick shower and slip
into something fashionably cute before Tinjin would
be knocking at her door. Excitement bubbled like a
fountain in the pit of her stomach, her knees quivering from her frazzled nerves. For the first time since
forever she was anxious for everything to be perfect. No man before Tinjin had ever been that lucky.

Stepping beneath the spray, Natalie relished the
flow of warm water over her skin. Her bodywash was
a Bath & Body Works treasure she'd brought back
with her from the States. The scent was Japanese
Cherry Blossom and with its hint of pear and san-
dalwood everything about it screamed luscious and
sexy. So much so, she'd purchased the body lotion
and the perfume and was set on slathering both over
her skin before slipping into the little black dress
she'd selected to wear for dinner. She took a deep
inhale and imagined the delicate scent teasing Tinjin's nostrils. A smile bloomed full and wide across
her face and she giggled, the sound echoing about
the space.

When she'd scrubbed every curve and crevice of
her body she wrapped a plush white towel around
her torso and hurried back to her bedroom. Minutes later she stood in front of her floor-length mirror, assessing her reflection. She'd pulled her hair
up into a loose ponytail. Her makeup was simple,

the barest hint of eyeliner, mascara and a nude lip gloss decorating her face. And the bohemian-style dress was perfection, complementing her lean figure. She partnered the simple cotton frock with a pair of beaded flip-flops.

She suddenly pulled at the elastic that held her hair in place, allowing the thick tresses to fall down to her shoulders. She pulled her fingers through the locks, shaking her head. She stared at herself, sighed heavily, then reached for the hairbrush that rested on her dressing table. Just as she finished redoing her ponytail the doorbell rang, the loud jingle announcing Tinjin's arrival. A wave of panic crossed her face as she stole one last glance in the mirror and headed for the front door.

Hesitating, Natalie took a deep inhale of breath, her hand shaking as she reached for the doorknob. She didn't know why she was so nervous, just wanting everything to be perfect when he saw her again. She paused and took a step back, then rushed into the kitchen to check on the meal. The bell rang a second time.

Tinjin stood anxiously outside the front of Natalie's luxury home. The neighborhood's reputation was one of affluence, the area known for its large Victorian townhouses and high-class shopping and restaurants. He stared out at the view of the impeccably manicured park across the way. The sun was beginning to set and the warm, humid air promised storms that would wash away the heat and bring some much-needed coolness. Glancing up one side of the street and down the other he couldn't help but note the casual, aristocratic atmosphere outside the woman's front door. His friend Gnat was living well, he thought to himself.

Tinjin was casually dressed in black slacks and a white dress shirt open at the collar. He held on to a bottle of wine with his left hand, his car keys twisting nervously in his right hand. It had been a long day and although he could feel the onset of jet lag in his muscles he was excited at the prospect of spending time with Natalie. Missing her when they were apart was beginning to take on a life of its own, the emotion corporeal as it swelled through his heart.

When there was no answer after he'd rung the bell for the third time, he pounded the door with his fist, the harsh rap reflecting his anxiousness. He was prepared to knock again when Natalie finally pulled the door open.

"Hi!" she said, fighting to keep her tone calm and even.

Tinjin grinned, his broad smile filling his face. "Hi!" he responded as she welcomed him inside.

"You're late," Natalie stated as she closed and locked the door behind him.

He shook his head. "I was early. You took forever to answer the door and let me in."

Tinjin leaned to press a soft kiss against her cheek. He eyed her intently as he pulled back, passing the bottle of wine into her hands. The faintest of flutters tickled Natalie's midsection.

She took a deep breath and held it before shrugging her narrow shoulders. "I really didn't take that long," she said, meeting the intense stare he was giving her.

Tinjin nodded. "You did, but I understand."

She gave him a curious look. "You do?"

"I'm thinking you had to get the food out of the take-out boxes and toss them into the trash before you let me in."

Natalie laughed. "Really?"

"Why else would it take you so long to answer the door?" He chuckled softly.

She narrowed her gaze. "I'll have you know I cooked. From scratch, cooked."

"That remains to be seen," Tinjin said teasingly.

Natalie waved an index finger in his direction. She pointed to her dining-room table. "Sit down and when you're done apologizing, TJ, I might let you slide," she said as she headed back to the kitchen.

Tinjin laughed heartily as he moved to the dining room. His gaze flitted around the space as he took in the view. Natalie had been right about her home being museumlike. The artwork was spectacular and much thought had been given to its presentation. Taking in the decor, he was duly impressed, something about the space still feeling warm and inviting. Everything about her home was reflective of the woman he was getting to know.

The dining room was exquisite. Polished wood furniture, oversize upholstered chairs and a large, beveled-glass chandelier decorated the space. A five-panel abstract oil painting floated against the neutral-toned walls. The image reminded him of the Greek shoreline at dusk. He leaned in to study it more closely. From the other room he heard the distinct rattle of pots and pans, a gentle tinkle of glass, and a low cuss word murmured under Natalie's breath.

"Everything okay in there?" he asked, his voice rising above the soft lull of music that played in the background.

"Everything is fine, thank you!" Natalie called back.

Tinjin smiled, continuing his tour of her personal possessions. The dining table was mahogany and round, a piece of art itself. Tinjin drew his hand slowly over the polished finish, admiring the craftsmanship. "Hey, I really like your table!" he called out.

"Thank you! It's a Fletcher Capstan table," Natalie called back.

"Really?"

He could sense her nodding her head. "After dinner I'll show you how it expands," Natalie said as she suddenly moved to his side. She carried a glass baking dish that she set on a heat pad that rested table center.

"It's really the coolest thing," she continued, excitement flooding her words. "It's a spinning kaleidoscope of wood that will double its seating capacity. It's truly a brilliant masterpiece of carpentry and geometry. I absolutely *love* this table!"

Familiar with the British luxury furniture maker, Tinjin laughed again. "Must be nice. The only other Fletcher Capstan table I've ever seen was on a private yacht."

Natalie pulled the oven mitts from her hands. "What private yacht?"

"The Vanessa-Lynn out of the British Isles. It's owned by a good friend of mine."

"Ernesto Vega is a friend of yours?"

Tinjin grinned. "A good friend. We go way back and I was best man at his wedding. How do you know Ernie?"

Natalie shook her head from side to side. "I've walked in two of his shows," she said, acknowledging the star dress designer. "And his wife and I modeled together many years ago."

"Vanessa doesn't model much anymore. Not since the baby was born."

Natalie gestured for Tinjin to take a seat. "Talk about a small world!"

His head bobbed up and down against his broad shoulders. "Theirs was the first table I ever saw. I played with it for almost an hour I was so intrigued!"

"The first time I saw that table I had to have one. Ernesto put a word in for me with the builder."

"I'm sure you still paid a pretty penny for it."

She nodded. "Had to do some print work I really didn't want to do," she exclaimed, "but I got my table!"

Tinjin chuckled softly as she turned in an about-face and exited the room. After returning to the kitchen twice more, Natalie finally took the seat across from him. The table settings were elegant, Natalie's best china and crystal atop woven place-mats. The meal was baked spaghetti, an amalgamation of pasta, sharp cheddar cheese and fresh tomatoes, partnered with garlic bread and a tossed salad. She dished both their plates then bowed her head as he said grace and blessed the meal.

As they dove into the food, the anxiety both had been feeling earlier seemed to dissipate. Conversation came effortlessly, reminiscent of their time together in the United States. They soon learned that for everything they had in common, there was much they didn't agree on. Tinjin's favorite color was green, hers was red. He loved meat and she could have easily lived on a vegetarian diet. Their debates were animated and filled with laughter. By the time Tinjin had shoveled down his third plate of food, he couldn't imagine that there was much more that he hadn't told her about himself.

Natalie was feeling the same way. Tinjin was easy to talk to and there was no subject off limits. They found a nice balance with each other, a comfortable give-and-take that worked well. She liked that he made her laugh and that his wisecracks came almost as fast as her own. She found herself grinning as he stabbed at the last bite of his spaghetti with his fork.

"Do you always eat that much food?"

He swiped at his mouth with an oversize paper napkin. "I do when the food is good."

She clapped her hands excitedly. "I told you I could cook!"

Tinjin's smile was expansive and intoxicating. He nodded his head. "I have to admit it. I'm very impressed. This was really good."

"How good was it?"

"So good that I owe you an apology."

She grinned back. "You owe me more than an apology!"

Tinjin watched as she rose from her seat, gathering the empty dishes. The back of her dress was open, exposing her warm brown skin. The design dipped low toward the arch of her buttocks. His eyes followed the line of her spine down to the luscious curve of her backside. Unable to resist, Tinjin gave the round bubble a light smack that made Natalie yelp in surprise.

He lifted his brow as she cut her eye at him, giggles erupting from her midsection.

"Excuse you!"

"I couldn't help myself," he said with a slight shrug and a self-assured smile. He leaned back in his seat, crossing his extended legs at the ankles. "So," he said with a quick pause, "what's for dessert?"

Natalie rolled her eyes. "I thought we already had this conversation?"

"We did and I distinctly remember you promising me something sweet."

"I don't remember the conversation going like that."

"My memory is clearly better than yours."

There was a pregnant pause between them as they stood staring at each other. Tinjin's gaze was narrowed as he eyed her seductively. His tongue slipped past his lips, grazing the flesh slowly. Natalie bit down against her bottom lip, a wave of heat flushing her face. She took a quick step back and turned abruptly.

"I guess I better get you some dessert, then," she muttered as she rushed out of the room, clearly unnerved.

Inside the kitchen she stood in front of the open freezer door, fanning herself. She was overwhelmed by the heat that had consumed her, needing every ounce of a cool breeze to stall the desire that had surged with a vengeance. When she was able to catch her breath she moved to the counter, prepping two dishes with a decadent confection.

Outside it had begun to rain, the downpour coming fast and furious. A bolt of lightning split the sky and seconds later the home vibrated with thunder. More lightning and more thunder flashed outside the kitchen window.

"Do you need a hand?" Tinjin suddenly asked.

Natalie jumped, not having expected him to step into the room behind her. She turned as he moved in her direction, his smile washing over her like the sweetest breeze.

She shook her head as she turned, a bowl extended between them. "Your dessert," she said as she passed it and a spoon toward him.

Tinjin laughed. "This looks good," he said, eyeing the large slice of hot peach pie that rested in a pool of warm vanilla custard. "It looks very good!"

"I don't know why you keep acting like I don't know what I'm doing in the kitchen. I told you this would be a meal you'd never forget."

Savoring the first bite Tinjin couldn't take his eyes off her. Her face was flushed, her cheeks tinged a warm shade of red. Joy and laughter danced in her eyes. She was intoxicatingly beautiful. He suddenly felt drunk with desire and they'd had nothing stronger than lemonade to drink.

Standing together they finished the last of their treat, neither saying a word. Each spoonful was slow and deliberate, their taste buds awash with pleasure. Natalie wanted to say something, to find words that would alleviate the erotic tension that had risen between them. But her mind was blank, nothing but thoughts of Tinjin and the heat of his touch washing over her. She took a deep breath and held it.

As if on cue Tinjin stepped in closer, trapping her between him and the countertop. Moving against her Tinjin dropped his bowl into the stainless-steel sink behind her, then wrapped an arm around her waist and pulled her against him. He lingered for a brief second before capturing her lips with his own.

Natalie closed her eyes tightly, falling into the moment. His kiss was sweet, like the sugary dessert they'd just finished. Tinjin tasted like cinnamon and nutmeg and vine-ripened peaches. His lips danced against hers, his tongue eager and searching as it slipped past her lips, caressing her tongue. He held her tightly, his hands gently stroking the line of her back, his fingertips burning hot against her flesh. It felt like heaven to be in his arms again. She felt his mouth graze the flesh of her neck. It was the softest of touches.

"I should help you with the dirty dishes," Tinjin muttered against her ear.

Natalie felt her pulse quicken, her body responding to the soft whisper on her skin.

"Oh…I…" Natalie managed to blurt out. The words caught in the back of her throat as Tinjin drew his hands across her torso. She arched her back as she felt his fingers trail gently over her body, wishing his hands were already beneath her clothing.

"Or we can do the dishes later," Tinjin mumbled, his tongue lapping at the dimple beneath her chin.

The sensation that swept through her body was overwhelming. A low hiss spilled past her lips, Natalie unable to form a coherent sentence. She had fallen into a daze, unable to reason what to do or how to do it. She pressed her hands against his chest and pushed him from her. They were both panting heavily.

"We shouldn't," Natalie gasped, "we should… we…"

"What?" Tinjin questioned, his tone a loud whisper. "What should we do?"

Natalie sucked in a big breath of air and swallowed hard. "We should move this to someplace more comfortable," she said as she grabbed his hand and pulled him along behind her.

Natalie led the way to her bedroom. The room was draped in white from floor to ceiling. White furniture, white bedding and white walls. Turning, she gave him a bright smile as she crooked her finger and gestured for him to come closer. Seduction shimmered in her light eyes as she gave him a come-hither stare.

Tinjin grinned back, every muscle in his body tightening with pleasure. He took two quick strides toward her, until her manicured fingertips pressed against his breastbone. Before he could say a word she pushed him down on the mattress. His eyes widened in surprise, the tables turning as Natalie took control.

Climbing atop his body, Natalie straddled him, her dress rising up her bare legs. She pulled at his shirt, releasing it from the waistband of his slacks, and slipped her hands beneath the fabric, gently raking her nails against his flesh. Tinjin gasped, air catching in his chest as she stroked his torso, her small hands massaging the taut muscles. Her mouth met his once again, the kiss drawing them closer and closer.

He cupped his own hands around her buttocks, his fingers meeting bare flesh and the thin line of her G-string. Heat surged into his southern quadrant, wave after wave sparked by him touching her bare flesh. He firmly gripped each cheek and felt Natalie shudder with pleasure as a slight jolt of electricity shot through her core. Her glutes were firm and tight, the skin unbelievably soft. He squeezed one cheek and then the other, then both at the same time.

Natalie's mouth clung to his as he touched her, his hands kneading her warm flesh teasingly. Everything about the moment had her craving him, desire raging through every nerve ending. Her desire was urgent as she suddenly pulled at his belt and undid his pants, tugging at the zipper. His own electrical current lengthened his erection, his manhood swelling with anticipation. Tinjin blew a low breath, a slight whistle falling past his lips.

Tinjin suddenly flipped her, dropping his pelvis against hers. Her hands raced down the length of his back, kneading every square inch of skin as she clung to him. In one swift motion he pulled her dress up and over her head and unsnapped her bra. His face dropped down between the fullness of her breasts and he suckled one hardened nipple and then the other, back and forth, his tongue lashing at her flesh.

His touch took her breath away and Natalie found

herself gasping heavily for air. Just as she thought she couldn't take another moment of his touch, her body convulsing with pleasure, he eased one hand between her legs, the other supporting his weight above her. He snatched her G-string from her body, ripping the string from the little weft of fabric that held it together. He threw it to the floor, then eased his fingers to her slit, the heat from the moist cavity leading the way. His thumb pressed hard against her clit and he rubbed it gently as he painted a trail of kisses across her jawline.

Tinjin fingered her gently, her knees sprawling open to allow him easy access. She moaned loudly as he eased two fingers inside her, his hand gently pumping into and out of her sweet spot. Natalie gasped loudly as Tinjin suddenly drew back, pulling himself from her. The heat gave way to a light breeze blowing between them, the chill startling every nerve and muscle in both their bodies.

Moving back onto his feet, Tinjin pushed his pants and briefs past his hips to the floor. He stood in full glory, wearing nothing but a raging hard-on and dark socks. He was lightly ripped, his muscles bulging and creasing in male perfection. His engorged member pushed forward like a snake that had been charmed into submission, awaiting the perfect moment to strike. He was nicely endowed and Natalie found herself salivating at its potential.

Her deep stare further fueled Tinjin's raging desire. He met the intense stare she was giving him with one of his own. She appeared both angelic and devilish as she lay sprawled against the bedspread, her naked body quivering with excitement. She was temptation personified, the embodiment of every-thing he had ever wanted in his lifetime and there, in that moment, she belonged wholeheartedly to him. "You are so beautiful!" he whispered, his words like the sweetest balm to Natalie's ears.

She pointed to the nightstand drawer and Tinjin knew what he would find inside. Pulling it open, a new box of Trojan condoms rested in front. He ripped the cellophane from the box and pulled one out. As he crawled back onto the bed, easing his body against hers, Natalie took the prophylactic from his hand and tore open the wrapper. She lifted her body enough to wrap her hands around his manhood, taking the wealth of him into her palm. His shaft extended from a nest of tight black curls. It was long, full and dark, his skin the color of rich, black marble. His flesh was soft and smooth, his organ feeling strong and delicate in her hand. She could feel his pulse beating rapidly beneath his heated skin, throbbing in perfect sync with her own heartbeat. She sheathed him quickly.

Bracing his weight on both hands Tinjin hovered above her, his body perfectly aligned with hers. He stared down into her eyes, his own misting slightly. Everything in him ached for her, his wanting so in-tense that he felt as if he might combust from the intensity of it. Staring into her eyes he could sense that she was feeling the same way about him. She pressed her hand to the side of his face, the pads of her fingertips gently caressing him. He dropped forward and captured her mouth beneath his. His kiss was possessive and needy, his craving dancing over her lips.

Natalie touched his face, in awe of how beautiful the man was. She was mesmerized by his stare, intrigued by what she saw in his eyes. He eased his body between her legs and entered her easily. Their joining was the sweetest union either had ever known before. He settled himself against her, his pelvis tight to hers. Both closed their eyes, savoring the sensations that came with the intimate touch.

His was a slow and steady pulsing, an easy in and out as he played her body like a master musician plays his instrument. He stroked and caressed her until she purred, eliciting the sweetest sounds from her. Her body pulsed around his, her taut muscles drawing him deeper and deeper inside her. She met him stroke for stroke, the two in near perfect sync as they found a comfortable rhythm with each other.

Natalie suddenly screamed his name, her nails digging into the flesh across his back. She screamed and Tinjin screamed with her, both falling right off the edge of ecstasy. Heat swarmed, the intensity of their coming volcanic. Every muscle in both their bodies convulsed and twitched, the tremors feeling as though they were never going to end. Falling against her Tinjin gulped air, struggling to catch his breath. Beneath him Natalie panted and huffed, desperate to fill her own lungs.

Minutes later Tinjin rolled to his side and pulled her close, cradling his body around hers. Skin kissed skin, slow, easy caresses, as they relaxed against each other. As the throes of their loving settled Natalie giggled softly.

"I hope you know this doesn't mean anything," she said, a sardonic teasing to her tone.

Tinjin laughed as he gave her a gentle squeeze. "Girl, please! You and I both know this means everything!"

Chapter 11

Hours later Natalie and Tinjin were still together. Laughter rang through the bedroom. They'd made love, napped, talked and had made love again and again. Despite the late-night hour both felt invigorated, thoroughly enjoying everything about their time together.

"You should consider yourself very special, TJ," Natalie said as she laid her body atop his and snuggled down against him.

"And why is that?"

"I have never let any man stay the night. Ever."

"That's good to know."

"Like I said…special!"

"I'll own that. Nothing I didn't know already,

though." He pressed a damp kiss to her forehead as he tightened his hold around her torso.

Natalie let out a low sigh as she stole a quick glance toward the clock on the nightstand. "What time do you need to get going?" she questioned.

Tinjin shrugged. "I don't have anything scheduled. I only need to make a few calls to get my move scheduled and finish some paperwork for the business."

"Are you excited?"

"About moving?"

"All of it. Moving, starting your own design house, me!"

Tinjin laughed as he nodded. "I am. It's been a lot in a short period of time but I don't think I'd have it any other way."

"Most especially me, right?"

He smiled. "Most especially you."

"I was just checking."

"Since you're checking, have you ever thought about living in Paris?"

Natalie lifted her head to stare up at him. She shrugged. "No. I haven't."

"Maybe you should."

"That sounds serious."

"I am serious. I don't do long-distance relationships well and something tells me you don't do them at all."

This time Natalie laughed. "You do know me well."

"So would you consider moving with me to Paris?"

There was an awkward pause as Natalie gave his statement some serious consideration. She pulled herself upright, leaning back against the headboard. "I would prefer we shelve this conversation until we are both fully clothed. I can't think clearly with you naked."

Tinjin sat upright with her, pulling the sheet up to his waist. "That's fair, but we will have this conversation, Gnat."

She leaned her head on his shoulder. "I need to get some sleep. I have a meeting in a few hours with Jourdan Claude."

"The new shoe company?"

"You've heard of them?"

"I consider them one of my biggest competitors. They've only been around for a few months and they're making great strides."

"I'm interviewing their management team for *Pretty, Pretty.*"

Tinjin smiled as he reflected on her comment. He didn't say anything, leaning instead to kiss her lips, gently whispering her name against her mouth.

Natalie wrapped her arms around his neck and kissed him back. "But I'm never going to get any sleep if you keep kissing me like that," she murmured when they finally came up for air.

Tinjin chuckled warmly. "Who needs sleep?" he replied as he plunged his mouth back to hers one more time.

Natalie felt as though she was in a daze. She and Tinjin had been going strong for weeks, spending every waking moment with each other. Where they laid their heads at night depended on what side of town they found themselves after the dinner hour. Some days she woke up in Tinjin's bed, other days she woke up in her own. They'd found a nice balance with each other and still hadn't discussed what would happen after his impending move to Paris.

She blew a deep sigh as she shifted her body against the canvas backdrop in the room, lights overhead burning hot and a camera flashing in her face. She was wearing a couture gown of ivory silk with red lacquered metal and ostrich feather embellishments. It was a lavish design and she wore it like a second skin. The photographer on duty gestured with his camera, directing her to drop her chin and give him more face. After complying she gave him pose after pose, bombarding his enthusiasm with fuel.

"That's it!" he exclaimed. "That's the money shot!"

Behind him Tinjin gave her a thumbs-up, his own smile contagious. Natalie smiled back, the gesture animating her light eyes. Her face glowed and the camera ate it up. Minutes later, the photographer yelled "that's a wrap" and they were done and finished for the day, everyone excited about the outcome.

"Hello!" she said as she threw her arms around Tinjin's neck. "This is a surprise."

He kissed her lips and hugged her tightly. "I finished my meeting early and thought I'd surprise you."

"I'm glad you did," Natalie said. "I didn't think I was going to see you tonight."

"Are you finished for the night?"

Natalie shook her head. "I have a dinner meeting in an hour."

Tinjin winced slightly. "You did tell me that. It went right out of my mind."

"When do you fly to Paris?"

"Tomorrow afternoon. But I'm only there a few hours to tour the factory, then I fly right back here for investor meetings."

"Still no takers?"

"Not one who's willing to meet me on my terms, but let's not talk about that. I don't want to jinx anything."

"What about the guy you met when you got back from the United States? Shouldn't he have given you an answer by now?"

Tinjin sighed as he thought about Jean-Paul Vivier. "He's a bit eccentric. I really have no expectations of him other than to expect nothing."

"What about the Dallas Stallions? Have you spoken to any of my cousins and asked them for help?"

He nodded. "I've been able to get as far as I have because of their investment. John and his brothers were very generous. If I don't get another dime I would still be able to make it work, but that extra cushion would be nice to have. It would allow me to take a few risks with the fall and winter shoe lines.

And if I'm going to catch up to Jourdan Claude I'll need to take some serious risks."

"I don't think you have anything to worry about. Once your designs start rolling off the lines you'll run circles around Jourdan Claude. I wasn't all that impressed with their designers or their management team. You are so much better and I'm sure you'll be far more successful."

Tinjin leaned to give her another kiss. "From your mouth to God's ears!"

Natalie smiled sweetly. "I need to change and get going. Will I see you later?"

Tinjin shrugged. "That depends."

She leaned back on her hip, one hand falling against her waist. "On what?"

He lifted his eyebrows suggestively then winked an eye. Natalie rolled hers skyward.

"I am not your late-night booty call, TJ!"

He laughed. "You're the one who asked about seeing me later, remember? I'm the one feeling like a slab of meat right now!"

She grinned as she pressed herself and her couture dress against him. "And a mighty fine slab of meat you are!"

His touch was electric. The first time she'd wakened to Tinjin tasting her sweet spot Natalie had lost complete control, unable to fathom how she was only in his apartment and bed and not lost somewhere in the stratosphere. Because with each pass of his tongue, his mouth locked against the door of her secret spot, she found herself reeling with pleasure, her body floating sky-high.

She gripped the sides of his head, his mouth bobbing up and down between her parted legs. His tongue caressed her slowly as he planted damp kisses down one side of her slit and up the other. Every muscle vibrated in response, her whole body one relentless tremor that could not be contained. He wrapped his lips around her clit and sucked her gently, his tongue washing her in small circles. His mouth was heaven-sent and Natalie arched her back in response, the convulsions moving her to pull his face against her as she pushed her hips to meet his tongue.

Her sweet scent filled his nostrils. He'd awakened to an erection that had refused to be ignored, her body wrapped around him like a warm blanket. The nearness of her was difficult to resist, her nakedness igniting a roaring flame deep in the pit of his spirit. He'd been hungry for her, his thirst feeling insatiable. And so he'd tasted her, determined to eat his way to ecstasy.

Natalie suddenly bucked, her body vibrating with a mind of its own. She bucked and twisted until they found themselves in a classic sixty-nine position and then she took him into her mouth to return the favor. It had become their morning ritual, their days starting in extreme ecstasy, both yearning for the other until the wanting actually hurt.

Their orgasms erupted at the same time, both exploding in sheer pleasure. Natalie stroked him fast and hard as he spilled his seed over her hand and against her lips. He pushed himself into her hand and pulled out, driving himself back and forth across her palm. It was bliss and a near-perfect way to start their day.

Tinjin was past the point of exhaustion. He'd been running on full steam for days with no end in sight. As he navigated the rise of his new business, every ounce of his fortitude was being taxed. His time was rarely his own and his to-do list was miles long. His one and only reprieve was the time he was able to spend with Natalie.

Natalie. Every time he thought about her he found himself grinning foolishly. The woman had gotten under his skin, attaching herself like an extra appendage he didn't need but couldn't see himself doing without. He was so far gone that he couldn't begin to imagine life without her. More importantly, he didn't want to.

Everything about the two of them together worked, even in those moments when they didn't expect it to. Despite being annoying and spoiled she was funny and intelligent and she made him laugh when he least expected it. If Tinjin were honest with himself, she had his heart, despite his best efforts not to let her.

Tinjin shifted in his seat, glad that he'd been able to make the early evening flight. He'd been back and forth between London and Paris, business and his growing fondness for Natalie holding him hostage in both places. He'd been serious when he'd asked her about moving with him to Paris. He also understood her reluctance to answer. He'd been second-guessing the question since it had come out of his mouth, unsure if he was even ready for a permanent relationship with any woman. And then he thought about Natalie, understanding that she wasn't just *any* woman. There was something special about her and, being honest, he was wholeheartedly happy that she was his woman and he had no reservations about claiming her.

As the plane touched down on the tarmac, taxiing slowing toward the gate at London's Heathrow Airport he engaged his cell phone and dialed Natalie's number. She answered on the second ring.

"Hello!"

"Hey, what are you doing?" Tinjin questioned. She sounded rushed and was breathing heavily into the receiver.

"I was just about to head out the door. Where are you?"

"At the airport. I just landed."

"I thought you were staying in Paris tonight?"

"I changed my mind. I missed you."

There was a moment of pause. "I missed you, too," Natalie said, her voice a loud whisper on the other end.

"Where are you headed?" Tinjin asked.

"Dinner, then out with the girls. But I can cancel if you want me to."

Tinjin shook his head. "Of course not! No, go have fun. I can meet you later. I only flew back to get me a quickie."

Natalie laughed. "You're so funny, TJ, but I don't do quick."

"That sounds like a personal problem to me."

She giggled again. "Goodbye you!"

"I'll see you later."

On the other end Natalie took a deep breath and then a second as she disconnected the call. On the other side of the room Jean-Paul Vivier was eyeing her curiously.

"Who was that?" the man questioned.

Natalie met the look he was giving her. "None of your business," she answered. "Are you ready to go?"

Jean-Paul nodded. "I'm delighted you agreed to see me again. I've missed you, Natalia! I've missed you so very much!"

Tinjin ran by his house first. The sparse decor had gotten scanter since most of his belongings had been transferred to his new home in Paris. Checking up on the place had become ritual since he now spent most nights with Natalie. He felt himself fingering the key to her abode, the act subconscious as he thought about her. Eventually he might consider selling the space, but until he was absolutely sure that he had no reason to maintain a residence in London, he planned to keep it.

He blew a deep sigh. He didn't expect Natalie to drop everything for him but he missed her badly. And missing her had him wishing she'd given up her night with her friends to spend all of her time with him. There was nothing rational about the thought but he wasn't afraid to admit to himself that he was having some issues. He didn't see himself being that forthcoming with anyone else. He chuckled softly, the sound echoing around the room.

His cell phone suddenly chimed in his pocket. Pulling the device into his hand he acknowledged the caller ID with a warm smile.

"Hello!"

"Why haven't you called me?" his sister Tierra questioned. Her reprimand echoed over the phone line.

Tinjin laughed. "I just spoke to you last week!"

"How's Natalie? Things still good with you two?"

"Natalie is good. Natalie and I are still good. Thank you for being concerned."

"I am concerned. I worry about you all the time."

"I'm a big boy, Tierra. I've been tying my own shoes and combing my own hair since I was eight. If I remember correctly I was also tying your shoes and combing your hair back then, too."

"You know what I mean."

Tinjin smiled. "How are the kids?"

"Growing too fast. The baby is trying to crawl

already and we just registered Lorenzo for T-ball. Hopefully you'll get back to the States to see him play before the season is over."

"I'll plan on it. Uncle's going to need to give him some pointers!"

"I really wish you'd come back home. I hate that you're out of the country."

"Well, you and I both know that's not going to happen anytime soon. Paris is going to be home for a while."

"How does Natalie feel about that? Does she want to move to Paris with you or do you two plan to do the long-distance thing?"

Tinjin shook his head. "Natalie and I are making it work for now. We're taking things slow. Besides, I'm so focused on business right now that I can't give the attention to a full-time relationship that I would need to."

"Yes, you could. Travis and I did it when he was deployed. You make it work if you love each other."

"Who said anything about love?"

"Mama Dee! Who, by the way, is having some health issues so make sure you call and check on her."

"What kind of issues?"

"She's not taking her blood pressure medicine the way she's supposed to and her numbers have been too high. The doctor fussed her good yesterday. Hypertension is not something to play with!"

"Mama Dee knows better. She's putting herself at risk for a stroke or a heart attack."

"She does know better but she refuses to change her diet and she doesn't get enough exercise so she has to take her medication."

"I'm sure stress doesn't help, either."

"Mama Dee doesn't have any stress. She's the most stress-free woman I know. You and I together have more stress than she's had her whole lifetime!"

Tinjin laughed. "You're probably right about that. I love how that old woman just takes everything so easily."

"But back to what I was saying before. Mama Dee says you and Natalie are in love with each other but neither of you is willing to admit it yet. And our grandmother is never wrong!"

Tinjin was grateful that his sister couldn't see the blush of color that had warmed his cheeks. He would never have gotten a break if she could see the expression that crossed his face. "Well, I don't know about love but I'll say we like each other a lot. We'll just see what happens."

Tierra nodded into the receiver. "Well, don't mess it up, Tinjin. You know how you can do sometimes."

"Goodbye Tierra. I'll call you next week."

"I love you, big brother!"

"I love you, too!"

Disconnecting the call, Tinjin felt his pulse quicken. Yeah, what he felt for Natalie was love, but until he could get a handle on things no one needed to discuss it. He stole a quick look at his wristwatch. He had time to kill before Natalie found her way home. His stomach rumbled and he realized he'd not eaten since earlier in the day. He suddenly remembered a little bistro near Natalie's townhouse that she'd encouraged him to try. Since he was headed in that direction he couldn't think of a reason why now wouldn't be as good a time as any other. Taking one last glance around the space, he made his exit and locked the door.

Natalie had finished two glasses of wine and was working on her third. Jean-Paul had been going on and on about absolutely nothing since they'd been seated. She smiled politely but everything about her body language said she had no interest in being there. He was the only one who didn't seem able to catch the clues. Dinner had only come after his insistence, the man promising a business opportunity she'd not be able to refuse. Only because Jean-Paul had always served her well when it came to business had she agreed to join him.

She reached for her cell phone to check the time and to see if Tinjin might have sent her a text message but there was nothing. It was radio silence. No calls, no messages, no nothing. She blew a deep sigh before forcing herself back to the conversation Jean-Paul was having with his lonesome.

"I'm not sure what I plan to do but I'm sure it will

all work out," he said as he reached across the table for her hand.

"I'm sure it will," Natalie responded as she pulled her fingers from his, dropping her hand into her lap.

"I was very impressed with that piece you did on Jourdan Claude. They are definitely a company one should keep their eye on."

She shrugged. "I wish them well."

"I actually met Claude Von Brett, the owner. He and I have much in common. I liked his wife, as well."

"Jourdan's very sweet," Natalie said, her gaze skating around the small restaurant.

"I've been thinking about doing business with them. How would you feel about that?"

Natalie shifted her eyes back to his. "What kind of business?"

"They need a financial infusion and I'm looking to get more involved. I could make you the face of Jourdan Claude. It could be a brilliant marketing strategy."

Natalie stared at him, not bothering to respond. She reached for her glass and took another swig.

"We can talk about it more at my party tomorrow night," he said. "They will both be there. And I don't know if I told you, there's another young designer looking for a handout to kick his design business off, as well. I want you to meet him, to give me your opinion."

"I don't know if I'm going to be able to make your party," Natalie said. "I might be unavailable."

"You must be there," Jean-Paul insisted. "This party is to honor you." He reached across the table, grasping her hand a second time. He pulled it to his lips and kissed her palm.

Natalie let out another deep sigh as she gestured toward the waiter with her other hand, needing a refill of her wineglass.

Tinjin had been seated at a table on the opposite side of the room when he spied the two of them together. He bristled as he watched Jean-Paul Vivier suck Natalie's fingers into his mouth. Her snatching her hand away did nothing to ease the swell of jealousy that had surged through his spirit.

He took a deep breath. Natalie had lied to him. He had trusted that she was having a good time with her girls and instead she was being wined and dined by another man. He couldn't help but wonder—if he had not come back to London unexpectedly would she and Jean-Paul be sharing more than dinner?

He was just about to confront the two of them when the restaurant's door swung open, ushering in Frenchie, Leslie and Imani, the trio moving quickly toward Natalie's table. There was a brief conversation before Natalie rose from her seat and bid Jean-Paul goodbye. The four women were out the door quickly, raucous laughter echoing after them. Neither had bothered to look in his direction, Natalie not realizing that he was even there.

Tinjin tensed. The waitress hovered over him,

ready to take his order. He'd suddenly lost his appetite, his mind racing as he tried to put the pieces together. Natalie had left with her friends, so her lie was more a half-truth, conveniently leaving out her dinner plans with Jean-Paul. And what was the relationship between the two? Tinjin hadn't been aware that they'd even known each other. He had more questions than answers and just as he was growing weary of trying to figure it all out, Jean-Paul called his name.

"Tinjin Braddy! How are you?"

Tinjin met the man's outstretched hand, shaking it in greeting. "Jean-Paul, what a surprise." He then eyed the man.

"Yes, it is. Did my assistant contact you with the information about my party tomorrow?"

Tinjin nodded. "She did. I look forward to it. I hope you don't mind if I bring a guest."

"Oh, please do. It will be quite the event. Of course, I'll have made my decision about your business venture and it will be a wonderful opportunity for us to both announce our plans. I'm also excited to officially announce my engagement. You just missed my fiancée," he said as he tossed a quick look over his shoulder and pointed toward the door.

Tinjin felt himself bristle a second time. "Your fiancée?"

Jean-Paul nodded as he continued. "But you'll have the opportunity to meet Natalia tomorrow."

Tinjin felt his jaw tighten as Jean-Paul extended

his goodbye. "Have a good night," he responded as the other man waved in response.

The waitress was still eyeing Tinjin curiously. "Are you ready to order yet, sir?"

He shook his head. "I've changed my mind," he answered as he placed a twenty pound note onto the table. "This is for your troubles."

The girl's eyes widened at the generous tip. "Thank you, sir! But you really don't…"

Her last words fell on deaf ears as Tinjin rushed from the room, heading to Natalie's home to wait. Intent on getting to the truth.

"So, what do you plan to tell Tinjin?" Frenchie asked, her forehead furrowed.

Natalie shrugged her narrow shoulders. "I don't plan to tell him anything. There's nothing to tell."

Frenchie shook her head. "I think he might want to know about Jean-Paul's obsession with you."

Natalie rolled her eyes. "He's obsessed with himself, not me. Jean-Paul is a nonentity in our lives."

"So, what about his party tomorrow? Are you going?"

"I really want to meet Karl Lagerfeld. Don't you want to come with me?"

Frenchie shook her head. "Why don't you take Tinjin?"

"I might do that. You act like I don't want Tinjin and Jean-Paul to meet."

Her friend laughed. "You don't need to convince me."

Natalie sighed. "Take me home. I'm intoxicated and you're picking on me. I can see things going downhill between us and I don't want you to ruin our friendship."

The other woman laughed, mirth flooding the air around them. "Our friendship will be just fine. However, you have a problem on your hands and you don't even know it," she said. "You need to tell Tinjin. He doesn't seem like the kind of man who would appreciate his woman keeping secrets."

"I'm not keeping secrets."

"But you are his woman?"

"I…we…it's…" Natalie stammered. "It's complicated."

Her friend laughed. "It's going to get complicated if you don't do what you need to do."

Chapter 12

Frenchie's words echoed in Natalie's head for the entire ride home. When her friend had dropped her off at her front door she'd admonished her one last time. "Seriously, Natalie, Jean-Paul is a whole other degree of crazy. Good men like Tinjin don't do crazy well, especially when it comes to their girlfriend's ex-boyfriend. Take it from a voice of experience."

Natalie blew a deep sigh. Clearly Francesca Adams didn't know what she was talking about. Natalie had no interest in Jean-Paul, and since their history together had never amounted to much of anything she saw no reason for Tinjin to be given the details. Tinjin knew how she felt about him. At least, he should, Natalie thought to herself.

She took a deep breath and then a second as she steadied herself at the bottom of the porch. She loved Tinjin. She loved him more than she ever imagined possible. Everything about his presence in her life felt right. From the moment they'd met, him standing over her in the airport, she'd felt a tremendous connection to the man. Now, when he was gone, she felt broken, something important missing from her. Home was in Tinjin's arms and she wanted nothing more than to stay there for the rest of her days.

Jean-Paul could never measure up to a man like Tinjin Braddy and Natalie's connection with him had only been a stepping-stone in her career. Jean-Paul had a history of dangling things she wanted in front of her to gain her companionship. And Natalie had always been able to keep him at arm's length, never crossing the boundaries of friendship. Jean-Paul could only dream about sharing her bed. And having her heart wasn't a possibility. Whenever his demands became too much, she had always pushed him away. Sending him packing always had him wanting to do more for her. It had become a vicious cycle and Natalie suddenly knew that it was a carousel ride that she finally needed to get off.

The home was quiet. There was only one light on, a faint glow coming from the kitchen. She kicked her shoes off in the living room, pausing to inspect the papers Tinjin had dropped on the coffee table and floor. His talent amazed her and she smiled as she studied the detailed designs that bore his signature.

In her bedroom Natalie found Tinjin in her king-size bed, curled up on his side, the sheets and blankets pulled tight around his body. She smiled. His being there brought her a level of comfort she'd never known before.

She tiptoed into the bathroom to brush her teeth and wash her face. After slipping out of her clothes and into her nightgown she eased into the bed beside him and pressed her body against his back.

Lying there, Tinjin had been waiting patiently, questions racing through his head, confusion spinning through his heart. He didn't know what to believe about Natalie and Jean-Paul and he didn't want to believe the worst. He had heard her the moment her key had hit the door lock. As she'd moved through the house, his anxiety level had increased tenfold. He'd waited to see if she would shower, fearful that there was trace evidence of an indiscretion she needed to rinse away. But nothing in her nightly routine had changed, Natalie's behavior as predictable as always. His paranoia had been just that. As Natalie pressed her body against his, he tensed, holding his breath as he struggled to still the heavy pounding in his chest.

Natalie snaked her arm around his waist, teasing his abdomen with her fingertips. She pressed a kiss to the back of his neck, blowing warm breath across his skin. Tinjin inhaled deeply, filling his lungs with her scent.

"You're home," he said, his voice low as he tried to keep his tone even.

"I missed you," she whispered back as she kissed him again.

"Did you and your friends have fun?"

She nodded her head against his back. "I would have had more fun with you."

Tinjin took another deep breath and blew it past his lips. "So did you guys catch dinner first? Did you get a chance to eat?"

There was a moment of hesitation before Natalie finally answered. "I actually had dinner with an old acquaintance. You might have heard of him. Jean-Paul Vivier?"

"You two are friends?"

"Acquaintances. He's introduced me to a lot of people in the industry that have helped my career. Do you know him?"

"We've met."

"Then you know there's nothing to be impressed about." She tightened the hold she had on his torso as she gyrated her pelvis against his backside.

Tinjin ignored the gesture. "Did you two run into each other or something?"

"Or something. He called me this afternoon and asked me to meet him. Had I known you were coming home I would have turned him down."

"So you two don't have a relationship? You've never dated?"

Natalie giggled, her mind still clouded with drink.

"He dated me. I didn't date him. But it's nothing you need to be concerned about. That man means nothing to me. We had dinner, talked about him introducing me to the powers at Chanel who are looking for a new spokeswoman and then I met up with Frenchie and the girls. Now I'm home here with you." She drew a warm hand across his crotch and his muscle jumped to attention. "And your friend," she giggled.

Tinjin took a third deep breath, holding it a brief moment before blowing it back out. He turned, lifting his arms to embrace her. He pulled her close, relishing the warmth of her body against his own. He pressed his lips to her forehead, kissing her sweetly.

Natalie smiled, inhaling the sweet scent of his cologne as she closed her eyes and pressed her face into his chest. "I love you," she murmured, the words barely an audible whisper. Minutes later she was sound asleep and Tinjin was watching her slumber, thinking about how much he loved her back.

"My head hurts!" Natalie muttered as she pulled a pillow over her face, rolling her back against the mattress.

"You have a hangover." Tinjin laughed.

"I drank scotch. I hate scotch."

He eased his body back against the bed, pulling her into his arms. "Then stop drinking scotch!"

"It's all Frenchie's fault! She made me."

Tinjin laughed.

"Not so loud!" Natalie exclaimed.

What's on your agenda today?" he asked.

"For the next two hours I'm going to nurse this migraine. Then I have a meeting this afternoon with a vendor who wants to buy advertising space on *Pretty, Pretty.*"

"Are you going to Vivier's cocktail party?"

Natalie lifted one side of the pillow, meeting his stare with one open eye. "I was thinking about it. He promised to introduce me to Lagerfeld."

"Would you like to go with me?" Tinjin asked, his eyebrows raised.

"You got an invitation?"

He shook his head. "Why does that surprise you?"

"I didn't know you and Jean-Paul knew each other like that."

"Well, he invited me. He's the investor I was telling you about. The one I was waiting for a response from. He's promised to tell me tonight if he agrees to my terms."

"So you're the designer he wants me to meet!" She suddenly sat upright, wincing from the pain that surged through her head.

"He told you about me?"

"He just said there was someone new he was thinking about investing in. But he's also considering a deal with Jourdan Claude, which would definitely be a conflict of interest. So, he's either playing one or both of you, or he's up to something else."

"Now, that's interesting to know."

"I don't want you to do business with Jean-Paul,"

Natalie said, meeting Tinjin's deep gaze. "He's not a good fit for you. The man has no integrity."

"But you're friends with him?"

She shook her head. "He and I aren't friends."

Tinjin studied her face for a moment. He leaned to kiss her mouth. "I'll make you breakfast, then I need to run. I'm meeting with a leather distributor this afternoon."

"I saw your designs," Natalie said. "They're beautiful!"

Tinjin grinned. "I'm excited about them. I can't wait until the samples are finished and I can see them on your feet."

Natalie lifted both her legs upward. She wiggled her feet left and then right. "I can't wait to see them on my feet, either!" she said.

Tinjin ran a hand down the length of her leg. He tickled the backs of her knees as he pressed a kiss to her thigh. He shuddered, a chill racing through his body.

"You really are a tease," he said.

Natalie grinned. "You're the one with the hands. I'm not touching anything."

"You have a headache."

"It's not that kind of headache!"

He grinned back. "I've got to get to work. You are not pulling me back into this bed."

Natalie lowered her legs and parted her thighs. Her nakedness peeked from the bottom of her nightgown. She drew her index finger into her mouth, spinning her tongue across her manicured nail. Her gaze met the look he was giving her.

Rising, Tinjin pulled off his clothes and threw them to the floor. They didn't bother with foreplay. Towering above her, Tinjin entered her swiftly, burrowing himself deeply inside her. Natalie arched her back, pressing her shoulders hard against the mattress as she lifted her hips to meet him. Their loving was quick and dirty as he stroked her, in and out, up and down. His hands danced from one breast to the other as he squeezed the lush tissue, rolling the nipples between his thumb and forefinger. Natalie grabbed one hand and drew his fingers into her mouth, sucking each digit like a lollipop. The sensation tightened his muscles, his whole body weeping for release.

Tinjin suddenly pulled himself from her as he flipped her onto her stomach. He lifted her onto her knees and entered her from behind. With one hand pressing hard against the back of her neck, pushing her shoulders downward as he held her by the waist, pulling her buttocks against him, he slammed in and out of her. Her body pulsed with pleasure, the lining of her sweet spot like a vice around his member. Her orgasm came first, her convulsions inciting his. Natalie cried out, his name rolling off her tongue again and again. His body clenched tight as she continued to push against him, pushing and pulling until she had milked him dry. They fell forward together, Tinjin dropping the wealth of his weight against her.

They both panted heavily, the ripples of ecstasy refusing to let go.

The second time he entered her he loved her slowly, savoring every sensation that swept between them. He relished the connection that had become a lifeline for them both.

Hours later, when Tinjin rushed out the door, he wasn't thinking about his meeting with the supplier or the drawings he'd left sprawled across the coffee table in her living room. All that was on his mind was getting back to Natalie, her Stallion heart holding him hostage.

There was attitude registered all over Natalie's face. Jean-Paul stood in her living room with insolence spilling out of his eyes. An argument had come to an impasse, both determined to have their way.

"I do not understand why you are being so difficult," Jean-Paul hissed between clenched teeth.

Natalie snapped back. "No one's being difficult. I just refuse to be manipulated."

"This should be the happiest day of our lives, Natalia! I am trying to give you the world!"

"I didn't ask you to give me anything. There is no *us* and we are not going to have a life together, Jean-Paul. Sooner or later you're going to need to get that through your thick skull."

The man bristled. "I am opening doors for you, Natalia! You should show me more appreciation. No one will love you the way I love you."

Natalie rolled her eyes. She blew a heavy gulp of air past her lips. "Does it not bother you in the least that I'm not in love with you, Jean-Paul? That I have never loved you?"

He turned abruptly, crossing his arms over his chest. Jean-Paul said nothing as he ruminated over her comment. When he turned back to face her he could see the disdain across her face. He took a deep breath. "You have never allowed yourself to give me a chance, darling. All I ask is that you consider what we could have together, *ma chère*."

Natalie pursed her lips in a slight pout, annoyance clouding the look she was giving him. She knew that once Jean-Paul started with the terms of endearment, calling her sweetheart and honey in his native French, that he would soon be crying and begging for her favor. His theatrics were predictable and old.

"What do you want from me, Jean-Paul?"

"At least come to my party. Allow me to make the introductions I promised to make. Important people are expecting to meet you. You owe me that. Then we can talk more later. Maybe work things out between us and at least remain friends. Give me that."

Natalie reached for her cell phone. She pushed the speed dial number that would connect her to Tinjin. He answered on the second ring.

"Hey, are you busy?"

"I'm never too busy for you. What's up?"

"Are you still planning to go to Vivier's party?"

"Only if you're going with me."

"I will only go if you want me there with you. Are you coming here first or do you want me to meet you?"

"I can come get you."

Natalie smiled. "See you when you get here!"

She disconnected the call and met the disapproving look Jean-Paul was giving her. She pointed toward her front door as she moved in the opposite direction.

"Show yourself out, Jean-Paul. I have to go get ready for your party."

Jean-Paul's cocktail party included an eclectic mix of power players in the fashion industry. Both Tinjin and Natalie were acquainted or familiar with most of the individuals in the room. They arrived fashionably late, ensuring that their arrival was talked about. Side by side they were a stunning couple, both long, lean and meticulously attired.

The dress Natalie wore was a Tin-men special, a one-of-a-kind creation that Tinjin had surprised her with. It was a tailored one-piece pantsuit in a navy-blue-and-white block print that she had paired with six-inch neon green stilettos. The garment fit her to a T, complementing her slim build, and was the talk of the night. Tinjin was handsomely attired in one of his own suits, the navy blue silk partnered with a blue dress shirt and matching necktie. Gucci loafers adorned his feet.

They were noticed, and as they made the rounds,

networking with other power players, photographers and paparazzi snapped their photo. Both knew that before the night was out their images would be all over the fashion blogs and websites. It would be the best kind of free advertisement.

From the other side of the room Jean-Paul saw them enter together, arm in arm. There was a glow to Natalie's face that he didn't recall ever seeing before. When he saw her with that designer, Tinjin Braddy, he struggled to hide his surprise and keep a smile on his face. He strode quickly to their sides to greet them.

"Natalia! Tinjin! *Bonjour!* Welcome to my event!" He was annoyingly loud and his tone was a hint abrasive.

Tinjin extended his hand. "Jean-Paul, thank you for having us."

"It's my pleasure. And of course, I'm sure you know that Natalia is one of my very favorite people!"

Tinjin eased a possessive arm around her waist and gently pulled her against him. He leaned to kiss her forehead, pressing a damp kiss to her skin. "She is mine, as well," he said as he locked eyes with the man.

Both could see Jean-Paul bristle, jealous anger washing over his expression. The man took a deep breath, fighting to contain his emotion. "Natalia, you didn't tell me you had a personal relationship with Mr. Braddy."

Natalie pressed a warm palm against Tinjin's

chest. "I didn't tell you because it's none of your business, Jean-Paul," she said, a bright smile on her face. She tilted her head ever so slightly, aware of the cameras pointed in her direction.

There was a noticeable twitch over Jean-Paul's eye and he clenched his fists tightly together at his sides. He twitched and then nodded his head. "Well, I need to go greet my other guests. You two enjoy your evening," he said as he turned abruptly and rushed toward the other side of the room.

Tinjin and Natalie tossed each other a quick look. "That was almost pleasant," he said.

"That man can't be trusted," she responded. "Don't turn your back on him because if he gets the opportunity he will stab you in it. One day I'll tell you about some of the things I've seen him do."

Tinjin laughed. He kissed her mouth. "I'm not worried about Jean-Paul," he said.

Natalie smiled as she hugged him close. Despite her casual expression, she couldn't help but think that they needed to worry.

An hour or so later Natalie and Tinjin stood in conversation with the team from Chanel. Laughter rang warmly as Tinjin told a joke. Both were making a very nice impression. The moment was interrupted when Jean-Paul called for everyone's attention, moving to the front of the room as he waved his hands in the air for silence. They all turned to hear his speech.

After thanking them for coming and extolling the talents of all in the room, he gestured to a man and woman standing off to the side to join him at the podium. He introduced Claude Von Brett and his wife Jourdan.

"Ladies and gentlemen, it's really my honor to announce my recent partnership with Jourdan Claude. I will officially join the team as director of artistic development and we're excited about the new line we will soon be bringing to you."

Tinjin sighed. He muttered in a loud whisper. "I guess I just got my answer about his investment."

"You don't need his money," Natalie said matter-of-factly. "I'll give you whatever you need. I'll be your partner."

Tinjin's neck snapped as he turned to stare down at her. "Do you know what you're saying?"

She nodded. "You want a line of credit. I happen to have a few million in the bank just earning interest. Consider credit given. In return, I'm the official face of Tin-men for Her—clothes and shoes. We can hammer out the rest of the details later. Deal?" She extended her hand.

There was a moment of pause as Tinjin stared at her, his eyes bright with wonder. He took her hand in his. "Deal!"

The two broke out in warm laughter as Tinjin wrapped her in a deep bear hug. His kissed her cheek, then her lips, oblivious to the attention they were getting from the crowd around them.

Jean-Paul interrupted the moment. Having concluded his speech he'd left the podium and made his way to stand beside them before either realized it. Natalie jumped when he cleared his throat to get their attention.

"Tinjin, I regret that I'm not going to be able to invest in your little shoe business," Jean-Paul announced loudly. He quickly looked over his shoulder to the audience watching and grinned.

Tinjin widened his stance, his body tensing slightly. He smiled politely. "Congratulations on your deal with Jourdan Claude. I wish you all much success."

"Oh, we will be successful," Jean-Paul said. His voice dropped to a low whisper. "And while that's happening I plan to destroy you!" he hissed between clenched teeth. "I promise you that. If it's the very last thing I do I will make sure your little shoe line never sees the light of day and any little glimmer of hope it might have will be discredited. When I'm done, your name won't mean anything in the fashion world. You're already a has-been and you don't even know it." He turned to Natalie. "When you're ready to be back on top, playing in the big leagues, Natalia, call me. I might be willing to take you back."

As Jean-Paul walked away, the whispering began and Tinjin and Natalie both sensed it wasn't going to stop anytime soon.

Chapter 13

Jean-Paul Vivier was methodical in his plot to take down Tinjin Braddy. He hit him hard and below the belt, his reach greater than Tinjin or Natalie wanted to believe. Frustration furrowed Tinjin's brow as he slammed down his cell phone, sending the device shattering to the ground. Natalie blew a low breath of air past her lips.

"So what do we do now?" she questioned.

Tinjin tossed up his hands. "What can I do? There isn't one supplier willing to sell me the materials I need. It's like he's blackballed me from here to the States and back. I can't get leathers. I can't get suede. Nothing! And the few places that have been willing to sell to me have jacked the prices up past the point of ridiculous. I'll never be able to make any shoes within a reasonable budget at those prices.

"Add in the fact that I have an entire plant that's not operating but costing me money and employees who are ready to jump ship. Every day that goes by things just go from bad to worse."

Enraged, Tinjin threw a punch at the wall. "Aargh!"

"We're going to get past this," Natalie said. "We're not going to let Jean-Paul beat us."

Tinjin shook his head. "You don't understand. My entire life savings is going up in flames. There are people who trusted me with their investments and right now I'm watching their money go up in flames, too. I don't know if I can get past this."

"We still have my money."

"What sense does that make?" Tinjin questioned, annoyance flooding his face. "Why would I throw good money after bad? I can't borrow any more money when I don't know how I'm going to pay back what I already owe."

"Let me make some calls," Natalie said. "I'm sure I can get some help from somewhere."

Tinjin rolled his eyes, not an ounce of confidence registering on his face. He didn't bother to comment, instead moving back to his computer as Natalie proceeded to dial the few friends she thought might be able to offer them some advice. Desperate to get his mind off his current situation he began to scroll through the daily fashion sites that kept him in the know.

It was a *Women's Wear Daily* feature that captured his attention. As he read through the article, his jaw tightened and perspiration beaded across his brow. From where she sat Natalie could see him becoming visibly distressed. He suddenly jumped from his seat, gasping for air.

"What's wrong?" Natalie asked, jumping with him. "Are you okay?"

"My designs!" he said, pointing toward the computer screen. "They stole my designs!"

Natalie moved to where he pointed, the headline announcing the launch of Jourdan Claude's new shoe line. The assemblage had been photographed in a room full of toddlers, a half-dozen little girls playing dress-up as a collection of stylish shoes littered the floor around them. Each pair had come directly out of Tinjin's portfolio.

"How did they steal my designs?" Tinjin shouted, ire flooding his spirit. "Those are my designs!"

Confusion washed over Natalie's face. "I don't understand…" she started.

"What's not to understand? I designed those shoes, not Jourdan Claude. Every one of those designs is mine!" He slammed back into his seat and resumed the slideshow one more time.

"This is not happening to me," Tinjin shouted, rubbing his eyes and brow with the palms of his hands. "God, why is this happening to me?" he muttered.

"I can call him," Natalie said. "I can call Jean-Paul and demand he stop."

Tinjin tossed her a look. "What? Why would you call him? Why would you want…?"

"I'm just trying to help," Natalie snapped. "Jean-Paul used to listen to me."

Tinjin bristled. "Did he? Because you were the only other person to see those designs. You had access to my work. I trusted you." He suddenly slapped his forehead. "Foolish me! I left those designs here with you. Did your friend manage to get my creations into his pocket with help from you?"

Natalie became indignant. "First, he's not my friend. Second, I've never given you any reason to not trust me. I didn't give Jean-Paul your designs."

"When was the last time you saw him?" Tinjin questioned.

Her eyes skated back and forth as she contemplated the question. She took a deep breath. "It was a day or two after his party. He just showed up here at the house."

"You didn't think to tell me about that?"

"You were in Paris. And there was nothing to tell. I let him say what he had to say and then I sent him packing." Natalie sighed deeply.

"You let him say what he had to say. And what, pray tell, was that?"

Another deep breath rushed past her lips. She thought back to her last encounter with Jean-Paul. He'd come begging, desperate to make amends with her. Despite the conversation having been heartfelt, Jean-Paul's apology seeming genuine, she'd been skeptical, her past experiences with the man leaving her cautious. But she hadn't told Tinjin, knowing it would have led to the argument they were now having. Her instincts had told her to tell him the minute Jean-Paul had left her home but she'd shrugged the encounter off, wanting to believe that it was done and finished for good.

Natalie became defensive. "Don't yell at me."

"I'm not yelling!" Tinjin shouted. "What did your boyfriend say?"

She stood up abruptly. "If you want to have a conversation with me then you talk to me like you have some damn sense. I have never shouted at you so you will not shout at me. And he is *not* my boyfriend and you know it!"

Tinjin's face was red with rage. Steam seemed to billow off his skin. "Did you give Jean-Paul copies of my drawings?"

"Are you really asking me that?"

"Did you leave them where he could see them?"

Natalie shook her head in disbelief. "I didn't leave them anywhere. If anyone left them exposed, it was you."

"This was *our* home. I thought I could trust leaving my stuff here and not have it stolen by the company you keep."

"Excuse you, but this is *my* home. You're a guest."

Tinjin bristled. "So it's like that?"

Natalie dropped her hands to her hips. Her own anger did nothing to stall every vile emotion spinning between them. "You moved to Paris, remember?"

Tinjin nodded, his head bobbing up and down slowly. He reached for his jacket. "I'll make arrangements to get my personal belongings out of *your* home," he snapped as he headed for the door.

Natalie called after him, unable to fathom how they'd gotten to the point of no return. "Tinjin!"

Saying nothing, Tinjin rushed out the door. He didn't bother to glance back in her direction, leaving Natalie to stand there in complete dismay.

"You stole his designs?" Natalie stormed into Jean-Paul's office, ignoring the assistant and the security person that tried to stop her. "What kind of monster are you?"

Jean-Paul waved off his staff members, gesturing for his secretary to close the door. He leaned back in his leather chair, clasping his hands together in his lap. Amusement painted his expression. "I don't know what you are talking about, *chérie*," he said. "Tell me what has happened."

"You know what happened. You stole Tinjin's shoe designs and you gave them to Jourdan Claude to pass off as their own."

"That would be industrial espionage," Jean-Paul said with a smirk. "How can you think I'd do such a thing? Is that the kind of man you think me?"

Crossing the room Natalie slammed her leather handbag against the desk top, marring the polished wood. "You came into my home and you stole from me. You can lie all you want but I know you did it."

Jean-Paul narrowed his gaze. He thought back to what he had done. Discovering Tinjin Braddy's drawings lying on the coffee table in Natalia's living room had been a moment of revelation for him. Her connection to the young designer had felt like a slap in his face, most especially after everything he had planned for the two of them. He'd been convinced that he could sway her to him, his wealth, power and connections significant motivators for many women. But Natalia had refused to be moved. Her throwing her relationship with the man in his face had been the last straw. If he couldn't have her, then the man who did had to suffer the consequences of her choices.

It had only taken a brief moment, when Natalia had left the room, for him to snap multiple photos of the drawings with his iPhone. Partnering with Jourdan Claude had only been the means to an end. Cutting off Tinjin's supply lines had given him enough time to bring those drawings from concept to completion. Now, if Tinjin were able to make those shoes, his would be branded as knockoffs and Tinjin a designer with no fresh ideas of his own. He knew that it would take little more to bleed the man completely dry, his financial resources shriveling considerably.

Jean-Paul leaned forward, cutting an evil eye in her direction. "I told you I would destroy him. You should have believed me."

Tears sprang to Natalie's eyes. "How can you say

you love me, then want me to be hurt? I don't get that."

"I never wanted to hurt you, Natalia, but you needed to see that he doesn't deserve you. You deserve a rich, powerful man who is going to look after you and take care of your every need. You needed to see that he is nothing. He's beneath you. I can give you the world."

She moved her head slowly from side to side. "I love him. He is everything I have ever wanted in a man. It's you who's beneath me. You don't come close to being a quarter of the man Tinjin is. You're a liar and a thief and I hope you rot in hell," she concluded.

Jean-Paul laughed. "There are worse things that could happen to me than rotting in hell," he said. "Just ask your lover!"

Natalie was hopeful as she dialed Tinjin's number for the umpteenth time. Since storming out of her home he hadn't taken any of her calls and he had not bothered to return her messages. She wanted to be angry that he was angry with her but instead she found herself overwhelmingly sad. And hopeful that if she kept trying, he would eventually come around.

She couldn't begin to figure out how to fix what was broken between them. Never before had any man been able to get under her skin the way Tinjin was, every thought of him like a bad virus with no cure. She missed him. She missed him so much that it hurt, the loneliness like nothing she'd ever experienced before. His distancing himself from her was devastating despite her best efforts to pretend otherwise.

She disconnected the line when it went to voice mail. There was no point in leaving a message Tinjin would probably just ignore. The sadness that washed over her spirit was ravenous. It was thriving and nothing Natalie tried made it go away. She was lost in thought when the notification announcement chimed on her cell phone. She read the message quickly, then moved to her computer, booting up the device.

Minutes later Natalie heaved a deep sigh. It felt like there was no end to just how low Jean-Paul was prepared to stoop. Now he was giving interviews, disparaging Tinjin's name and hers. Her fellow fashion bloggers couldn't wait to share the information with her, notification after notification chiming in the background.

As she read the indictment of Tinjin's talents and her abilities, her own ire rose with a vengeance. There would be just enough interest to get people talking and enough people talking that any condemnation of them could impact their reputations. And she wasn't having it. Both she and Tinjin had worked too hard to go down without a major fight. And if Tinjin wouldn't hear her out, she knew people who would. Moving back to her phone, Natalie dialed and waited for her international call to connect.

Tinjin's Paris home was located in the super-chic eighth arrondissement or administrative district of France's capital. Situated on the right bank of the Seine and centered on the Champs-Élysées, the eighth was one of Paris's main business districts. It was central to the best shopping and dining that the city had to offer and he loved its classic Parisian vibe and energy.

Pacing the hardwood floors, he couldn't begin to know why he was there, alone and miserable, missing Natalie with every ounce of energy he had in his soul. It had been weeks since he'd stormed out of her home and had left London, still furious about the theft of his work.

Pure rage had fueled their last argument. Rage and hurt that everything he'd been working so hard for was falling apart before his eyes. Despite knowing deep in his heart that Natalie had done nothing to purposely hurt him, he'd blamed her anyway and all because of her ties to Jean-Paul Vivier.

He blew a deep sigh as he moved from one end of the living space to the other. Minutes later his new cell phone rang, vibrating harshly against the kitchen table. He didn't bother to look at the caller ID. His most recent calls had all been bad news and despite Natalie's best efforts to reach him, he'd refused to answer, unable to find the words to apologize and still stinging from the hurt of everything that had happened to him.

He wasn't expecting the doorbell to ring, and when it did he jumped, caught off guard. Moving to the front of the home he peered past the curtains of the front window to peek out at the front stoop. His eyes widened in surprise as he rushed to the door and pulled it open.

His sister Tierra and their grandmother both stood with their hands on their hips, their no-nonsense expressions greeting him. Matthew Stallion stood behind them, a sheepish grin on his face.

"Why didn't you answer your phone?" Tierra said in greeting as she pushed her way inside. She hugged her brother close, kissing his cheek.

"I like this!" Mama Dee exclaimed as her gaze swept over his living space. She patted his chest with a warm hand. "This two bedrooms or three?"

Matthew laughed as he extended his hand and shook Tinjin's. "It's good to see you again."

"What's going on?" Tinjin questioned, surprise and confusion still blanketing his expression. "What are you all doing here?"

"Natalie called us. Now I'm here to rescue my investment," Mama Dee said. "Where's the kitchen? I think better when I'm cooking."

Wide-eyed, Tinjin pointed and his grandmother followed the line of his finger, disappearing toward the back of the home.

"Natalie called and told us what was going on," Tierra said. "You should have called us, big brother! Why didn't you call us?"

Before he could answer, Mama Dee stuck her head back into the room. "I need you to go to one of those nice vegetable markets I saw and pick me up a few things. And call my future granddaughter-in-law and tell her I'm here so she can come meet me. Tell her dinner is in one hour."

Tinjin shot them all a look. "Mama Dee, Natalie is in London. There's no way she can get here to Paris in an hour."

Mama Dee chuckled softly. "I know where Natalie is. And if you answered your phone you would, too. Now call her."

Matthew was still grinning from ear to ear. He gestured with his head. "Why don't I go to the market with you and explain what's going on," he said. Mama Dee shot him a look and something like fear passed over his face. "After you make that call, of course," he added.

The old woman gave them both a quick nod of approval as she moved back into the kitchen. "Tierra, you come give me a hand, please. Give your brother a minute to get his bearings."

Tierra kissed Tinjin one more time. Her own eyes were wide as she met the look he was giving her. "Be afraid," she whispered. "Be very afraid!"

"Now, Tierra!" Mama Dee called, her booming voice echoing through the space.

Once the two men were out of earshot, both burst out laughing.

"Your grandmother is a pistol!" Matthew exclaimed.

"You don't know the half of it! So what's going on?"

"Natalie called and explained what was going on.

She knew Stallion Enterprises has some resources here and thought we might be able to help."

Tinjin shook his head. "Wow! And I have been such an ass toward her."

"We all have our moments. But she loves you and even with you acting a fool she hasn't given up on your love. Good women are like that."

"I need to make this right."

Matthew laughed. "I don't think you're going to have any problems with that. Something tells me that if it's the last thing she does, your grandmother is going to make sure you make things right!"

Mama Dee's grocery list was a lengthy inventory of fresh vegetables, baguettes and condiments that Tinjin had not yet bothered to purchase. As he selected tomatoes and peppers Matthew gave him a quick update.

"Before I leave I will connect you with Pierre Demy. He's the senior solicitor in Stallion Enterprises' European offices and he's based here in Paris. He was instrumental in negotiating our import deal with the French Trade Commission so he has a multitude of contacts and resources at your disposal." Matthew passed him a business card with the man's contact information before continuing.

"Natalie said you were having difficulty finding vendors willing to supply you with material so Pierre has already taken care of that. You now have a line of credit with the top vendors worldwide that Stallion Enterprises will guaranty, so all you need to do is start ordering what you need. She also gave us the evidence that was needed to bring a lawsuit against Mr. Vivier. It's a good thing you sign and date all your original drawings. Our legal team is going after him and Jourdan Claude hard. There might even be criminal charges brought against him. If nothing else, the publicity alone will cast some doubts on how he and they do business." Matthew paused, taking a deep breath before speaking again.

"I've also got my people ensuring that your permits and your plant are ready when you are. What we can't do, however, is give you new designs to work with. That's on you, brother."

Tinjin shook his head. "I don't know what to say. You're taking a risk."

"We don't think so. My brothers and I are pretty selective about where we invest our money. We have all the confidence that this will inevitably be a win-win situation on both sides. I personally reviewed the numbers on your clothing line and you've had some impressive growth, despite your transition and focus on women's accessories. You've been smart. You built a solid management team. You managed your money wisely. There's nothing any of us would have told you to do differently. We're impressed and we're excited to support men like you."

"How do I begin to thank you?"

Matthew laughed. "You'll get our bill. But right now you need to call that woman of yours. I'm not explaining to your grandmother why she isn't there when dinner gets served."

When Tinjin opened his front door to let Natalie in, it took everything in him not to drop to his knees and sob. He stepped out on the front landing, wrapping his arms around her. He pressed his face into her hair and inhaled her scent, every sweet memory flooding over him.

"I'm so sorry," he whispered into her ear, tears pressing hot against his eyelids.

Natalie clung to him for only a brief moment before pushing him away. She shook her index finger at him, her stoic expression giving him reason to pause. "I'm still mad at you," she said as she pushed past him into the home.

Mama Dee stood in the foyer eyeing the two of them. A wide grin filled her face as she extended her arms toward the young woman. "Aren't you just the prettiest little thing," she crooned as she wrapped Natalie in a warm hug.

"It's so nice to meet you, Mama Dee!" Natalie intoned as she hugged the matriarch back.

Behind them Tierra waved, clapping her hands. The two women embraced, greeting each other like old friends.

"Come on in and have a seat," Mama Dee intoned. "This boy got a pretty living room. Whole house just pretty!"

Tinjin watched as they left him standing with

a foolish look on his face. Matthew shrugged, his shoulders pushing toward the ceiling. He shook his head. "Women!" he whispered under his breath as they both fell in line and followed them.

Dinner was an amalgamation of comfort foods. Mama Dee had prepared a vegetable lasagna laden with squash, carrots, mushrooms, onions, bell peppers and three different cheeses. The fresh baguettes melted in their mouths and dessert was her famous strawberry shortcake made with hot, homemade biscuits, fresh-picked berries and whipped cream. Tinjin and Matthew both sat in the shadows, the women controlling the conversation as they got to know each other better.

Every so often Natalie would focus her gaze on him, staring at him intently, but not once did she utter a word to speak to him directly. Despite his best efforts to engage her in conversation she would not be budged and neither his grandmother nor his sister tried to give him a hand or plead his case. He shook his head, recognizing that he now had three women in his life who could hold a grudge with the best of them.

Matthew interrupted the reverie. "I hate to eat and run, ladies, but I need to head back to the airport. I have to be back in Dallas in the morning."

Mama Dee nodded. "Thank you again for everything you were able to do for my grandson. I just need one more favor from you, though."

"Anything, Mama Dee," Matthew responded.

"If you would please drop me and Tierra off at our hotel, please. I need to get me some beauty sleep. It's been a long day!" She tossed Tinjin a look. "We're staying at the Hotel San Regis! Travis picked it out!"

Matthew smiled. "Not a problem, Mama Dee. It would be my pleasure."

"I need to be leaving, too," Natalie said, moving onto her feet.

Mama Dee laughed. "Baby, you ain't going nowhere. You and this boy need to make you some plans, like when you gone move to Paris 'cause y'all wasting too much money flying back and forth to see each other. Tinjin's gonna be on a tight budget until he start selling some shoes so y'all gone need to figure out how you plan to make it work. You two need to talk and make up. Tomorrow, I want to go shopping and buy me a pretty dress from Paris so I'm gone need your help!"

"Yes, ma'am," Natalie answered, looking a touch flustered.

Tierra laughed. "You get used to it."

Matthew nodded. "You do!"

Hugs and kisses ended the evening as everyone said their goodbyes. Matthew promised to follow up with Tinjin later in the week. As the door closed behind them, an uncomfortable quiet flooded the room. Staring him down one last time Natalie took a deep breath, then left him standing in the center of the living room as she moved into the kitchen to clear away what remained of the dishes.

An hour later Tinjin found Natalie sitting on the foot of his bed, staring out into space. He dropped down beside her, saying nothing as his broad shoulder brushed gently against hers. They both sighed at the same time.

"You really hurt my feelings," Natalie finally said.

Tinjin nodded. "I apologize. I was wrong and I know it."

"I would never have betrayed you like that."

"I know. I was angry and I took it out on you. It should never have happened."

"I really like your grandmother. She's been very sweet to me."

He smiled. "She likes you, too."

Natalie nodded. "I think she should move to Paris and live here with us."

Tinjin paused. A slow smile pulled at his full lips. "So does that mean you're moving here to Paris?"

"I like this place. You have good taste."

He chuckled ever so softly. "Thank you for helping me," he said. "I'm amazed at everything you did."

"I told you it would work out. You should have trusted me."

He took a deep breath. "I do trust you. I hope you know that."

"I know that we have a lot of work to do, both personally and professionally. And I know that we can get more accomplished together than we can apart."

"I love you, Gnat!" Tinjin said as he reached for her hand, entwining her fingers beneath his own. "I love you so much!"

Natalie's smile was wide and bright. "Tell me something I don't know, TJ Braddy!"

Chapter 14

Natalie's smile widened as Tinjin stood and moved to the fireplace. Minutes later the flickering of flames dimly lit the room and the soothing crackling of firewood was all that could be heard. She stared as he made a quick exit, returning moments later with a bottle of expensive champagne and two crystal flutes.

"I'd bought this to celebrate the release of the new Tin-men designs. But I think we now have that and so much more to celebrate," he said. He popped the cork and poured one glass and then the other.

She took a sip of the bubbly beverage as she met his gaze. "So now that we're back in business, what's next?"

Rising once more he moved to the worktable that

sat in the corner and pulled a stack of papers into his hands. "What do you think?" he asked, sharing his latest artwork with her.

As she flipped through them Natalie's eyes were bright as she nodded her approval. "These are amazing! They're even better than your last collection. I love the uniqueness of the heels!"

"I think these will get us some attention. Hopefully we can go into production in the next two weeks and the rest will be history."

"We have a lot of work to do. You have production issues to arrange. We need to schedule photo shoots, get a marketing plan in place and talk to potential buyers. We have a long to-do list."

"So you plan to be a very hands-on partner?"

"Extremely hands-on!"

His face gleamed with joy. He leaned to kiss her mouth, allowing his lips to linger against hers. His whispered breath was hot against her skin, sending a wave of heat coursing through her body. "I like it when you say *we*," Tinjin muttered against her mouth. "I really like that a lot."

They spent the next hour talking, plans interspersed with more apology as both strived to fix what had been cracked. Tinjin knew that they were back in balance when Natalie's wisecracks came fast and furious. Laughter returned, easing the last ounces of hurt away.

With the bottle of champagne finished Tinjin held her, the two lying back against the mattress as they traded easy caresses, reacquainting themselves with what had been lost for what felt like forever. Natalie was putty as she melted beneath the look in Tinjin's eyes. She was also toasty from the champagne and his stare served to heat her even more.

Tinjin eased his hand against her face, his fingertips gently caressing the line of her profile. She had to be the most beautiful woman in all the world, he mused as he stared. He kissed her again and again, painting her with damp kisses, his lips like the finest brush against her skin. Moving his mouth to hers, he danced his tongue past her lips, inside the moist cavity. She tasted sweet, her essence a permanent marker seared deep into his spirit. The kisses went on for an eternity, both savoring the sweet sensations the touch elicited from their bodies.

Natalie suddenly pulled herself from him, throwing her legs off the side of the bed. Rising she turned to face him as she slowly unbuttoned the white blouse she wore. She undid each pearl button slowly, exposing just the barest hint of brown skin little by little.

As he watched her Tinjin felt himself harden in his slacks, his manhood rising to magnanimous proportions. The bulge pressing against the fabric was taut to the point of pain, a sweet sensation that had him yearning for more. As he watched her continue her slow striptease he pulled at the belt wrapped around his waist and unzipped his pants, releasing the tightness confined inside.

Natalie smiled as her hands danced over her torso

and waist. She pulled her blouse off her shoulders and let it drop to the floor. Beneath the cotton garment she'd donned a white lace corset that slimmed her already thin waist and accentuated the lush curve of her breasts. Loosening the snaps she threw it aside. Her firm, full breasts seemed to leap free, standing at attention. She heard Tinjin gasp as her fingers skated across one and then the other, her fingertips resting where her nipples protruded like hardened candy waiting to be tasted. She found herself captivated by the glittering stare he was giving her.

Her skirt came next as she reached behind her to lower the zipper, allowing the silk pencil skirt to puddle around her ankles. The barest hint of fabric covered the sweet spot between her legs. She bent over at the waist and peeled down her silk panties. She felt him focused on her as she pulled the waistband down her flaring hips and past her knees. She soon stood in the center of the room, blushing to the roots of her hair, stark naked except for her heels.

Tinjin reached for her and she took a quick step back, avoiding his touch. She shook her head, then pressed her palm to his chest and pushed him away. As he fell back his manhood protruded forward, rising like a phoenix to be revered. He was hard and rigid, the turgid protrusion eagerly flexing for attention.

She took him into her mouth, her tongue lashing over the cushioned head of his organ. Tinjin gasped for air, the sensation of her touch blowing his mind. He couldn't talk, every muscle quivering for attention. She sucked him in and out past her lips, slathering him with the hot, wet moisture in her mouth. He lay back with both hands pulled over his head, savoring every sweet sensation.

As she held him in the palm of her hand Natalie felt him pulse and twitch, his desire surging. She suddenly released him, crawling up the mattress until she hovered above him. She met his gaze as he locked eyes with her, slowly lowering her body to his. The walls of her feminine spirit were tight and hot, and her inner lining pulsed and surged as she drew him deep inside.

Tinjin grabbed the bedclothes with both fists, the fabric clenched tightly between his fingers as Natalie began to ride him, up and down, round and round, over and over again. He thrust himself upward, desperate to meet her stroke for stroke, unable to contain the enthusiasm that had surged with a vengeance. With each push and pull he felt himself falling deeper into ecstasy until every nerve ending convulsed and his entire body seized.

Their loving lasted for hours, one orgasm after another flooding them both. Just when neither thought they could take any more, emotion swelled thick and full and more was all either craved. When the morning sun shimmered through the white lace curtains in Tinjin's bedroom, it found him tasting her, nourishing himself from the fountain of her secret garden. The intimate kiss started their morning and if it were not for both of their cell phones ringing at the same time, loving each other would have lasted the entire day.

Mama Dee had dictated the balance of their afternoon, her maternal interference both a blessing and a curse. She'd been bossy, nosey and abundantly loving to them both. Tinjin nodded as his grandmother admonished him, reiterating every life lesson she'd ever taught him and Tierra.

"You do right by that little girl, you hear me?"

"Yes, ma'am."

"Don't you be shacking up like you haven't been taught better, because you have been taught better. You love her. I could be dead and blind and still see how much you love her, so you do right!"

Tinjin tossed Natalie a quick glance. "Yes, ma'am!"

"And the two of you stop playing games with each other! I have never seen young people play games the way y'all do. Speak your mind, always tell the truth, learn to take criticism and be nice to each other. You don't always need to prove a point. It's okay to be wrong sometimes."

Tierra laughed. "Mama Dee, you sound worried!"

Their grandmother laughed. "I do sound a little anxious, don't I?"

Both Tierra and Tinjin nodded, eyeing her warmly. Tierra turned to give her brother a hug. "Take care of yourself, please. And if you need us, call! It's what family is for, Tinjin."

"I will," Tinjin exclaimed.

"I'll make sure he does," Natalie quipped, moving them all to laugh.

Matthew had arranged for the Stallion jet to take them home and they stood together in the private hangar at the airport, saying their goodbyes. As Tinjin watched his family board, joy and happiness shone in his eyes. He reached for Natalie's hand and held it. She stood by his side, her own excitement melding with his and both were grateful for the moment.

Jean-Paul's fall from grace came with little media attention. He took a plea deal for the criminal charges levied against him, and his ties to Jourdan Claude were terminated abruptly. The civil suit was settled quietly, both sides signing confidentiality agreements about the settlement. All anyone knew was that weeks later Tinjin Braddy had no problems settling every one of his debts. News of Jean-Paul's demise barely garnered two lines in the European papers and the last anyone heard he'd gone to Switzerland to lick his wounds.

Tin-men Designs was growing by leaps and bounds, much attention given to the new designer and his brand. The digital magazine *Pretty, Pretty* featured his story on its first cover, the article spinning Tinjin Braddy to a new level of popularity. When Natalie Stallion landed the cover of *Vogue* magazine wearing Tin-men, the notoriety of the brand was suddenly synonymous with those popular red-bottomed heels. Billed as a necessary staple for women with discerning taste, Tinjin's shoes were soon being photographed on the feet of every industry A-lister on multiple continents.

Tinjin and Natalie were flying private, the plane landing in Salt Lake City ahead of schedule. It would be the first break the couple had had since forever, business having occupied every waking moment and most of their dreams. Both were looking forward to the opportunity to spend time with family, and each other, it having been weeks since they'd been able to steal some real quality time together.

"You are not allowed to talk about business for the next three days," Natalie said. The expression on her face was intimidating.

Tinjin smiled. He lifted his hands slightly, his palms facing out as if he were surrendering. "No business. Three days," he said. "I promise."

"I mean it, TJ. You mention that shoe factory one time and I will hurt you."

"Okay, I get it," he said. He dropped his head into her lap, extending his legs against the leather seat. The flight was long and despite the exceptional comfort he was ready for it to be over. They had much to do in three days and Natalie didn't know the half of it.

Noah Stallion met them at the airport, watching from the observation deck of the private terminal as the charter flight taxied off the tarmac and into the hangar. The two men greeted each other warmly after Natalie had thrown herself into her brother's outstretched arms, hugging him tightly.

"How was your flight?" Noah asked, reaching to help with the luggage.

Natalie shrugged. "It was okay. I'm just glad to be home, though."

Noah gestured toward Tinjin. "How's business going?"

Tinjin shot Natalie a look, her eyes narrowing ever so slightly. A smile pulled at his lips as he met the other man's eye.

"I can't," Tinjin said, his head moving from side to side. "Your sister has threatened me with harm if I even think about business, let alone talk about it."

"And I mean it, too," she said.

Noah laughed. "Well, then, we can't have her drawing blood. I would really hate to arrest her."

"Do you have handcuffs?" Natalie suddenly questioned, curiosity washing over her expression.

"Of course, I do. But why would you be asking…?" Noah stalled, his words falling off abruptly as he caught the look his sister had thrown in Tinjin's direction. He shook his head. "That's just really too much information."

Tinjin and Natalie both laughed.

The afternoon was spent catching up with the rest of the family. Natalie enjoyed talking with her sister while Tinjin and her brother spent time together. She only hated that she would miss Nathaniel and Nicholas, who were both in Los Angeles.

Tinjin stared out the sliding glass doors as the two women strolled the gardens, both chatting away as if they might miss something. For the first time in weeks Natalie looked completely relaxed. He tossed Noah a quick glance as the man moved to his side to look where Tinjin was staring.

"She looks happy," Noah said, his tone casual.

"I try very hard," Tinjin replied. "I love your sister and her happiness means everything to me."

Noah nodded. "So things are working out for you both in Paris?"

"It is. Business is keeping us running but it all seems to be falling into place nicely."

"That's good. I'm glad to hear it."

Tinjin looked at Noah. "I'm glad we have this moment together. There's something I want to talk to you about."

"Do we need to take a seat?"

Tinjin shook his head. "When we first met I told you that it would be important to us for both of our families to support our relationship. I needed you and your brothers to like me, and my sister and grandmother would need to like Natalie."

"I remember," Noah interjected.

"Well, I know my family adores your sister and I hope that you and I are well on our way to being good friends because I want to ask your permission to marry Natalie. She has always looked at you as her father figure and I know how much it would mean to her to have you give us your blessing."

Noah stared back out the window, eyeing both of his sisters with sentiment. For a brief moment they were little girls again, laughing and dancing around the yard without a care in the world. And then he blinked, the extraordinary women they were staring back at him.

He turned and offered Tinjin his hand. "Natalie's not like any other woman you'll ever know," he said as the two men shook hands. "She pretends to be tougher than she is. She's actually quite sensitive and she requires a special touch. I hope you're up for the task."

Tinjin nodded. "I think I am. I love your sister with everything I have in me. I want to do right by her and I want to start by making her my wife."

"Then you have my blessing and I'm sure my brothers will support you, as well."

Tinjin grinned and waved a hand in Natalie's direction. She waved back, her own smile miles wide, nothing but love shimmering in her eyes.

It took some maneuvering but two days later Natalie and her siblings were being given a tour of Briscoe Ranch and the Stallion family home. Briscoe Ranch was well over eight hundred acres of working cattle ranch, an equestrian center and an entertainment complex that specialized in corporate and private client services. With the property being central to Austin, Houston, Dallas and Fort Worth, Briscoe Ranch had made quite a name for itself.

Back in the day, Edward Briscoe, the ranch's original owner, had been one of the original black cowboys. Not long after the birth of his three daughters, Eden and the twins, Marla and Marah, he and his first wife had expanded their Texas longhorn operation, adding two twenty-thousand-square-foot event barns and a country bed-and-breakfast.

After Marah Briscoe's marriage to John Stallion, Edward had gifted the property to his daughter and new son-in-law, her love for a Stallion ending the conflict that had bought the couple together in the first place. Under the Stallion family umbrella, Briscoe Ranch had grown substantially, specializing in corporate and private client services. It was also a point of consideration for a number of government programs, the property used to assist children and families in need. More importantly, the ranch was home to them all and the pride and joy of the Stallion clan.

Natalie was in awe of the wedding chapel, a charming structure built back in the late 1920s and since completely remodeled. She couldn't help but be impressed as they stepped through the double wooden doors and took in the beauty of the interior.

The cedar pews had been polished to a high shine, the coloration a rich mahogany red. Stained-glass windows shimmered color across the walls. A runner of red carpet atop the hardwood floors ran the length of the center aisle. It was going to make a perfect venue for a wedding.

"This brings back memories!" Tierra exclaimed as she leaned into her husband's side.

Travis nodded. "The happiest day of life before the births of our babies," he said.

Tinjin wrapped his arms around Natalie's shoulders. "It's not Paris but it's also home."

"It's perfect," she said as she reached up to kiss him, brushing her mouth gently against his. "It's absolutely perfect." She held out her left hand to admire the sapphire and diamond ring Tinjin had placed on her finger two days earlier.

The Utah Stallions all nodded their approval. Naomi brushed away tears of joy as she sat in a front pew, taking it all in. Her baby sister was getting married and the tears wouldn't stop flowing.

Marah reached for Natalie's arm and looped it through her own. "Let's go back to the main house and I can go over all the arrangements with you. We need to make sure we have everything you want because this is your day!"

Natalie's brothers moved to shake Tinjin's hand.

"Dude!" Nicholas said. "You sure about this?"

Noah laughed. "You're the only one scared."

Nicholas laughed with him. "Damn right! I know I'm not ready to head down this road. I'm just looking out for Tinjin."

Tinjin joined in the merriment. "I am absolutely sure," he said. "Your sister is going to make me the happiest man in the whole wide world!"

Chapter 15

The following morning Natalie Stallion and Tinjin Braddy professed their love and adoration, promising to love and honor the other until death parted them. Their commitment to each other was witnessed by family and friends just as the sun came gleaming through the stained-glass windows of the Stallion family chapel. The abundance of love there to support them was overwhelming and the happy couple couldn't have asked for a more perfect day.

Red roses and hints of baby's breath adorned the church and the bridal bouquets. Tierra, Naomi and Frenchie stood at Natalie's side. Travis, Nathaniel and Matthew stood by Tinjin. Noah walked his sister down the aisle.

Natalie wore a gown of antique lace designed by her husband. It was everything a girl could have wished for and more. She was stunning, everything perfect from head to toe. Side by side they made a beautiful couple and no one could begin to know the team they'd already become.

Tinjin married his best friend, vowing to support and protect her. His grandmother held his arm as he'd moved into place before the pastor, showing her support and solidarity. From her seat in the front pew, Mama Dee's affection for them all was magnanimous.

The reception lasted until the wee hours of the morning, the family dancing the night away. The sounds of laughter could be heard coming from an oversize tent that filled the yard. Natalie and Tinjin stood alone in the rose garden, holding tight to each other as they stared up to the late-night sky.

"Look!" Natalie exclaimed as she pointed to a shooting star streaking across the sky.

Tinjin smiled. "Did you make a wish?"

His new bride laughed. "I most certainly did!"

"Well?"

"Well, what?"

"What did you wish for?"

The beautiful woman paused for a brief moment. She turned in her husband's arms and looked into his eyes.

"What did you wish for?" he persisted.

She smiled sweetly. "Snow."

Momentary confusion washed over Tinjin's expression. "Why snow?"

Natalie laughed. "I was thinking it might not be so bad if we got stranded at the airport while we were on our honeymoon."

Tinjin stood staring at her, his eyes blinking rapidly. "Really, Gnat?"

She giggled. "My wish, TJ. Make your own if you don't like it."

He laughed, wrapping her in a deep embrace. He kissed her and she kissed him back. She was everything a man could wish for and both knew he would forever have her Stallion heart.

* * * * *

REQUEST YOUR FREE BOOKS!

2 FREE NOVELS
PLUS 2 FREE GIFTS!

KIMANI™
ROMANCE

Love's ultimate destination!

YES! Please send me 2 FREE Harlequin® Kimani™ Romance novels and my 2 FREE gifts (gifts are worth about $10). After receiving them, if I don't wish to receive any more books, I can return the shipping statement marked "cancel." If I don't cancel, I will receive 4 brand-new novels every month and be billed just $5.44 per book in the U.S. or $5.99 per book in Canada. That's a savings of at least 16% off the cover price. It's quite a bargain! Shipping and handling is just 50¢ per book in the U.S. and 75¢ per book in Canada.* I understand that accepting the 2 free books and gifts places me under no obligation to buy anything. I can always return a shipment and cancel at any time. Even if I never buy another book, the two free books and gifts are mine to keep forever.

168/368 XDN GH4P

Name	(PLEASE PRINT)	

Address		Apt. #

City	State/Prov.	Zip/Postal Code

Signature (if under 18, a parent or guardian must sign)

Mail to the **Reader Service:**

IN U.S.A.: P.O. Box 1867, Buffalo, NY 14240-1867
IN CANADA: P.O. Box 609, Fort Erie, Ontario L2A 5X3

Want to try two free books from another line?
Call 1-800-873-8635 or visit www.ReaderService.com.

* Terms and prices subject to change without notice. Prices do not include applicable taxes. Sales tax applicable in N.Y. Canadian residents will be charged applicable taxes. Offer not valid in Quebec. This offer is limited to one order per household. Not valid for current subscribers to Harlequin® Kimani™ Romance books. All orders subject to credit approval. Credit or debit balances in a customer's account(s) may be offset by any other outstanding balance owed by or to the customer. Please allow 4 to 6 weeks for delivery. Offer available while quantities last.

Your Privacy—The Reader Service is committed to protecting your privacy. Our Privacy Policy is available online at www.ReaderService.com or upon request from the Reader Service.

We make a portion of our mailing list available to reputable third parties that offer products we believe may interest you. If you prefer that we not exchange your name with third parties, or if you wish to clarify or modify your communication preferences, please visit us at www.ReaderService.com/consumerschoice or write to us at Reader Service Preference Service, P.O. Box 9062, Buffalo, NY 14240-9062. Include your complete name and address.

KROM15

Desire is more than
skin-deep

Moonlight *Kisses*

PHYLLIS BOURNE

It's just Sage Matthews's luck that Cole Sinclair, the man stirring her
dormant passions, wants to buy her cosmetics company. Takeover
bid: denied. But in the bedroom, their rivalry morphs into sizzling
chemistry. The kind of partnership Sage craves takes compromise
and trust—do they have the courage to go beyond the surface to
find what's real?

"A memorable tale of letting go of the past and taking risks. The
characters are strong, relatable and will inspire readers to carve their
own place in history." —*RT Book Reviews* on *SWEETER TEMPTATION*

Available May 2015!

www.Harlequin.com

KPPB4040515

Let love in…

KIMANI™ ROMANCE

Beautiful *Surrender*

Sherelle Green

An Elite Event

Mya Winters is organizing a charity date auction. There's one hitch: her cohost, private investigator Malik Madden, only has eyes for her. If she'd just confide in him, he could help piece together the truth about her past. But trust works both ways. And his only chance at a future with her is to share a secret that threatens their passionate connection…

"This story will make even the most skeptical person believe in fate and the idea of the universe working to bring two people together."
—*RT Book Reviews* on *A TEMPTING PROPOSAL*

Available May 2015!

H HARLEQUIN®
www.Harlequin.com

KPSG4030515

Harmony Evans

Winning Her Love

KIMANI ROMANCE

Winning Her Love

Bay Point Confessions

Harmony Evans

Bay Point mayor Gregory Langston wants community activist Vanessa Hamilton to help run his reelection campaign. Their attraction is a potential powder keg, especially when they are on opposite sides of a controversial issue. But a vicious smear campaign could destroy Gregory's shot at a second term. Will it also cost him forever with Vanessa?

Bay Point Confessions

"With endearing and believable characters whose struggles mirror real-life family dramas, the unique storyline captures the reader's attention from start to finish."
—RT Book Reviews on STEALING KISSES

 **HARLEQUIN®**
www.Harlequin.com

Available May 2015!

KPHE4020515